"Perhaps
Mickie

Barbara said.

"And go where?" Zack asked harshly.

"I don't know. Somewhere—far away. Somewhere…"

"Somewhere alone?" he asked. "Just the two of you? At the whim and mercy of a madman?"

"No," Barbara whispered. "Alone. But so far away from him that he wouldn't find us."

"And me, Barbara. Would I not be able to find you, either?"

"After all that's happened," she asked, "why would you even want to?"

Dear Reader:

News flash!

The Branigans Are Back!

All of you who have written over the years to say how much you love Leslie Davis Guccione's BRANIGAN BROTHERS will be thrilled and pleased that this rambunctious family is back with *Branigan's Break*.

More Fun from Lass Small!

We start the New Year with a fun-filled *Man of the Month* from one of your favorite writers. Don't miss *A Nuisance*, which is what our man makes of himself this month!

The Return of Diana Mars!

So many readers have wondered, "Where is Diana Mars?" This popular author took a break from writing, but we're excited that she's now writing for Silhouette Desire with *Peril in Paradise*.

Christmas in January!

For those of you who can't get enough of the holidays, please don't let Suzannah Davis's charming *A Christmas Cowboy* get away.

Mystery and Danger...

In Modean Moon's *Interrupted Honeymoon*.

Baby, Baby...

In Shawna Delacorte's *Miracle Baby*.

So start the New Year right with Silhouette Desire!

With all best wishes for a great 1995,

Lucia Macro
Senior Editor

Please address questions and book requests to:
Silhouette Reader Service
U.S.: 3010 Walden Ave., P.O. Box 1325, Buffalo, NY 14269
Canadian: P.O. Box 609, Fort Erie, Ont. L2A 5X3

MODEAN MOON
INTERRUPTED HONEYMOON

SILHOUETTE *Desire*®
Published by Silhouette Books
America's Publisher of Contemporary Romance

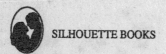 SILHOUETTE BOOKS

ISBN 0-373-05904-3

INTERRUPTED HONEYMOON

Copyright © 1995 by Modean Moon

MODEAN MOON

once believed she could do anything she wanted. Now she realizes there is not enough time in one life to do everything. As a result, she says her writing is a means of exploring paths not taken. Currently she works as a land-title researcher, determining land or mineral ownership for clients. Modean lives in Oklahoma on a hill overlooking a small town. She shares a restored Victorian farmhouse with a six-pound dog, a twelve-pound cat and, reportedly, a resident ghost.

Prologue

In her dream, he touched her. Just that; nothing more. A hand on her shoulder. Her throat closed and went dry as all the old longings, forbidden longings, rose within her.

She dared to look up at him, and for a moment she saw all the love she could ever hope for reflected in his eyes. But only for a moment. Then came fear, anger, possession, pain, and finally revulsion.

In the way of dreams, the hand, no longer his, tightened on her shoulder, forcing her to her knees.

The gun lay in its accustomed place on the floor beside her. Now the strange hand guided her own, forcing her to pick up the gun, forcing her to aim, forcing her to fire. And as he fell, destroyed by her, her hand, which was now the gun, her arm, her very self, disintegrated with the violence of the explosion.

Barbara whimpered once, then lay still, waiting for the images to fade from the darkness surrounding her. When they refused to do so, she released her pent-up breath in a quavering sigh and pushed herself up against the headboard, taking blanket and sheet with her, until she sat huddled in a tented cocoon, knees up almost beneath her chin, and stared out over the shadows of the strange, moonwashed bedroom.

She let out another long, shaky breath and forced her hands to release their death grip on the blanket. She'd read somewhere that symbolism, the language of dreams, was tailored by the subconscious of the individual dreamer, and she wondered if the rest of her was as shallow, as easily read, as the symbolism of her recurring nightmare.

She studied the unfamiliar shapes in the shadows around her. She didn't know why she did so; she was moving the next day and had no need to be familiar with this room.

Moving again. Sometime soon she was going to have to stop running, to find a place that could be her home, to rebuild her life. To find her way out of the nightmare.

One

─────

"We may have found her."

Zack Gordon raised weary brown eyes to the man seated across the desk from him. More than a year had passed since he'd last heard those words. That time, like all the others, had resulted in another fruitless search. "Your enthusiasm is overwhelming, Taylor."

"As is yours," Taylor Adams told him, a cynical lift of his eyebrow his only inflection.

Zack had hired Taylor as chief of security three years ago, after his relocation to Houston, long after Barbara's disappearance, so Taylor had never met the woman they now discussed in jaded terms. "Is there any reason for enthusiasm?" Zack asked.

"Maybe," Taylor told him cautiously. "I spent some time on this before I brought it to you."

Zack nodded, silently telling Adams to proceed.

"Damn it, Zack! It's too pat. The woman has fallen off the face of the earth, and a week after Truett surfaces, we just happen to get a tip on her whereabouts. Can they be working together?"

"No."

Ordinarily the quiet warning in Zack's voice would have stopped Taylor, but not this time. "This is too important, Zack, too dangerous for you, to be clouded by what you felt for this woman."

"She was an innocent," Zack told him. "Brilliant, but totally naive about the world. She'd spent all her time in classrooms and laboratories before we married. She'd never had a chance to grow up."

"A person can grow up awfully fast with the right incentives," Taylor said.

Zack closed his eyes, then opened them quickly against the images that flooded up from his memory. Taylor didn't know. And he ought to. For no one else would Zack reveal the pain of this admission, but Taylor needed to know who and what he might soon have to confront.

"Truett had her for two weeks before we were finally able to track him down. I received the first message from him before I even knew she was missing. In it, he promised to send her to me, a piece at a time, if I contacted the police. During those weeks, every day or so, he'd send me a videotape of her. There wasn't much on the tapes—at least not . . . at least not in length, but enough to let me know she was still alive . . . to show me some of what he was doing to her, and to tell me what he would do if I didn't give in to his demands. She was not a willing participant in anything he did to her."

"Christ," Taylor said on a slow breath, and Zack watched realization pale and silence the man.

"Let me see what you have," Zack prompted.

"Sure." Taylor shook his head, straightened in the chair, and once again was the seemingly unshakable man Zack knew him to be. "Sure." He handed Zack one of the two folders he held. "It's a quiet neighborhood. The pictures are the best we could get without making our man too conspicuous. We don't have an in-depth report yet. No sense in alarming the natives if this is another wild-goose chase."

Barbara was a small woman, less than an inch over five feet tall, and had always been slender. The woman in the first photograph was thin to the point of emaciation. She wore black slacks and a lightweight sweatshirt, both too large for her. Her honey blond hair, shining clean, had been pulled back into an unbecoming knot. The hollows beneath her eyes were too deep, her cheekbones too pronounced, the line of her mouth too tense.

"Has she been ill recently?"

"Not that we discovered."

There were other pictures. Zack sorted slowly through them. In one she was driving a new station wagon, apparently stopped at a light, her hazel eyes caught in a moment of introspection, thoughts turned inward, revealing a pain too great to look upon.

Barbara, Barbara, he thought. *What have we done to you? You were supposed to have made a new life for yourself, put me and what happened so far in the past that you can't be hurt. Why haven't you?*

"Get some security in place for her," he said.

"It's not another wild-goose chase, then?" Taylor asked.

Zack shuffled the photo to the back of the stack. "No."

The next picture showed Barbara standing beside the station wagon with several girls. Two stood next to her: one about ten, one much younger. He saw no pain in her eyes in this picture; he saw no emotion at all. "Who are the children?"

"Those two are in her household. Apparently she carpools the others to their private school one day a week."

"She's living with someone?" Zack asked, wondering at the sharp ache the question caused. Hadn't he just wished her to have made a new life?

"No." Taylor opened the second folder. "She's housekeeper for Meg Riley, a fairly successful Western novelist. Here's a feature article that ran in the Sunday magazine section a few weeks ago about her employer."

"A housekeeper?" Zack took the additional papers but didn't look at them. "A housekeeper? She has a Ph.D. in physics. What's she doing working as a housekeeper?"

"She's married to one of the richest men in this country," Taylor said, and Zack once again heard the cynicism that too often shadowed Taylor's voice when he spoke about women. "What's she doing working at all?"

Upstairs in his private files, Zack had the letter Barbara had left him. He'd found it on her empty hospital bed a month after the FBI had finally located her and he had been forced to wait helplessly on the sidelines while strangers stormed into the abandoned warehouse to rescue her, to wait and wonder if she still lived, to wonder if one of the many shots fired that night struck her, to wonder, as he had since she had been taken, how he had been so careless with her safety.

Never again would anything hurt her, he'd promised as he went into her room that night to tell her that at last she was well enough that he could bring her home. Instead he'd found an empty bed, and the note. He'd read the note, wadded it up, thrown it across the room, and then retrieved it.

Zack didn't need to read it again to know its contents, but once again he took it from the folder, spread it out and re-read it, touching the paper she had touched, seeing her fine, clear penmanship made spidery and all but illegible in places by emotion.

Dear Zack,

Thank God, you were not the one to have to kill someone. I don't think I could live with myself if you had been brought to that because of me.

Don't go after Truett. I want him dead, too. God knows I want him dead—but not at your hands. If you ever loved me, then please, I beg you, let the law punish him.

I thought I knew what loving you would mean. I was wrong—so wrong. I'm not a strong person. I can't live with the kind of fear I've been taught. Divorce me, Zack, for your sake and mine—

Her pencil had broken there, leaving a scarred line across the page, and she had left the letter unfinished and unsigned.

He'd gone a little crazy then, giving vent to the fear and pain that had gripped him for weeks. But it had done no good. Barbara Smith Gordon had, as Taylor had so aptly put it, fallen off the face of the earth, and nothing he'd done, no favor he'd called in, no investigator he'd hired, had given him any hope of ever seeing her again. Until now.

Zack had let Taylor talk him out of going after her today. And, in truth, Taylor's arguments might have been valid if any other woman were involved. Taylor's report said Barbara had been in Texas for three years. How much coincidence could there be in her moving to the affluent suburb where she now lived with her employer within weeks of his moving his corporate offices to Houston?

No, Zack hadn't gone after her, not because of Taylor's persuasion, but because of one picture: the one with the children; the one in which her eyes showed no emotion at all. As security chief, Taylor was paid to be suspicious. But then, he hadn't known Barbara before.

She had been young, eager, and glowing with enthusiasm when Zack had first met her. She had been hunched in front of a computer, studying wind velocity and air drag against wing structure when he'd made one of his periodic visits through his research lab. The visit had been made necessary by a design flaw in their new experimental executive jet. At a certain speed in the initial flight, the right wing had become unstable, and only the skill of the test pilot had averted a crash.

Zack was not happy, and while he more than appreciated a good-looking woman, his lab was not the place for youthful naiveté.

"I know you want answers, Zack," Ray Sanders, the design engineer, said tersely as they walked through the lab. "Hell, I do, too. The staff in the aviation department swore by this design. I'd be willing to swear by it, too. Everything checks out...."

"Except the damn thing won't fly."

Sanders sighed. "Except the damn thing won't fly." He veered to the right, stopping behind the slightly built girl seated at the computer. "But we're working on it. Barbara seems confident..."

At Zack's inquisitively raised brow, Sanders hesitated. "Barbara? Dr. Smith? She's been with us about a month." He tapped the girl on the shoulder, attracting her attention, and she turned with a frustrated frown marring the otherwise unlined freshness of her face.

"Zachary Gordon," Sanders said, "meet Dr. Barbara Smith, latest addition to your staff."

She looked about fifteen. Her short, honey-colored hair was a cap of riotous curls, and her hazel eyes were large and guileless behind a pair of enormous rimmed glasses. She wore no makeup, and her small figure was hidden beneath a shapeless lab coat. And she was either psychic or extremely perceptive, because she knew instantly what he was thinking.

"Oh, Lord," she said softly, grimacing. "Look. I'm twenty-two but..." She raked a hand across her forehead and started over. "I'm qualified...." She smiled ruefully and pointed to Sanders. "*He* hired me. *He* can tell you my qualifications." She held her thumb and forefinger a quarter of an inch apart. "I'm this close to some kind of answer, and if I lose my concentration, I don't know how long it will take to get back to this point." With that, she turned to the computer, obviously dismissing him from her mind.

Zack was reminded of Jack and the Beanstalk Giant, David and Goliath, and *The Little Engine That Could,* all at once. He felt a smile quirking and quickly blanked his expression. "Well?" he asked Sanders, but he moved a few steps away, so that their conversation wouldn't disturb her.

Sanders held up a hand, ticking off points on his fingers. "B.S. Summa cum laude, Massachusetts Institute of Technology. M.S., MIT. Ph.D., physics, Cal Tech. She helped design the computer software we've been using for the last two years as part of her doctoral dissertation. And the only way I hired her away from Lockheed was—one, we don't work with military aircraft or armaments, and, two, we're diversified enough to promise her more than aviation experience.''

Zack continued to watch her while Sanders spoke. Suddenly she blanked the graphics from her computer screen. Then the graphics were back: one jet in schematics, then a second. She activated the printer, then moved the schematics until they overlapped.

This is it, Zack thought. She's found something. He shifted slightly so that he could see her face as well as the screen.

''Ray,'' she said softly, summoning Sanders to her side. ''Here it is.''

Zack couldn't believe the transformation. The adolescent imp of a few moments before, the attractive woman he had taken a peripheral, irritated interest in when he'd first entered the lab—both were gone. In their place was a supremely beautiful, confident woman. Her eyes were dancing. Alive.

Zack dragged his thoughts from his memories to the photographs Taylor had brought him, to the note he held in his hand. It had taken too much for anyone to have to bear to kill the light in Barbara's eyes. And he had watched it happen.

Selfishly, he wanted to go after her this moment, lock her up in the compound that masqueraded as his home, and keep her safe. But he had failed to keep her safe in the past. And she had run from him because of that failure.

So for now he'd watch her, keep his protection in place around her, and wait.

Barbara had managed to stay on her feet until after Meg's fever broke shortly after three that morning. Then she had allowed herself a few hours' sleep. *Not many,* she'd promised herself, Dianne was still fretful with the aftermath of the particularly vicious strain of flu she had brought home from school, and Mickie, though resilient, was still weak. But a few hours... She needed that much if she was to be any good for the rest of the household.

She dreamed. The nightmare again. A measure of her exhaustion after three nonstop days of sickroom duty.

Swallowing tightly, pushing the horror of the dream to the shadows of her mind as long years of practice had finally allowed her to do, Barbara freed herself from the twisted sheets. The room was like an oven. But before she found the strength to crawl out of bed to adjust the thermostat, she felt a blast of cold air. Shivering, she pulled the sheet around her and huddled beneath it.

. . . With Truett.

"No," she begged. "Zack—help me. Please help me."

She saw Mickie's riotous red curls as the girl bent over her—the look of fear in Mickie's hazel eyes—felt the cool brush of a damp cloth on her forehead, then fell back into the nightmare.

"Why wasn't I notified?" Zack asked, breaking the tense silence in the car.

"You were—" Taylor braked to avoid a car that cut in front of them in the heavy afternoon traffic, then swerved around it "—just as soon as I was. Wilcox's team is good. I don't think there's a chance in hell anyone got past them."

"But no one answered the door?"

"No."

Damn it! Zack raged inwardly. Had he failed her again? Somehow, some way, had someone managed to get to her again? After seven years, his fear for her was just as great as in those first horrible days.

Taylor turned on to a quiet residential street and parked beside a van bearing a utility company logo. Instantly Zack was out of the car.

"Anything new?" he asked Wilcox, the first of the two men who approached him.

"No. As I told Adams, no one left the house yesterday, but we did see the subject outside for a few minutes in the late afternoon. There were lights on in the house until—" he referred to a small black notebook "—three-fifteen a.m. No one's been seen arriving or leaving since a drugstore delivery two days ago, and there's been no noticeable activity in the house. When I went to the door an hour ago, ostensibly for the gas company, no one answered the doorbell. That's when I called Adams.''

Zack stared at the sprawling stone house across the street, willing a door to open or a curtain to flutter, but neither did. The newspaper remained unattended on the flagstone sidewalk near the porch; the house remained ominously silent.

"You're sure no one went in?" Zack's words came out clipped and harsh.

Taylor shook his head. "You know as well as I do that there are ways to avoid surveillance. Our teams are thorough, Zack, but not infallible."

"Then I'm going in."

Taylor caught Zack's arm, stopping him. "It's not safe for you. Probably nothing's wrong, but if Truett did get past us—"

Zack shook off Taylor's restraining arm. "Then, go with me."

On the fourth ring of the doorbell, the door eased open a scant inch. Zack stepped back, searching to see past the crack in the door to who had opened it. Barbara? Was this to be the way he saw her for the first time in years, with fear and frustration darkening his expression and twisting his features. And she? How would she look? And how would she look at him?

But the voice, when it came, came from much lower than Barbara's would have. About his waist level, Zack decided, maybe lower. And the voice itself was as tiny as its speaker. "Who are you?" it quavered.

Zack closed a mental fist over his emotions and calmed his voice. "I'm Zack Gordon and this is—"

The door flew open, and he found himself staring down at three feet of determined girl-child, still clad in a nightshirt—an outrageous neon pink nightshirt that clashed with her unruly copper-colored curls. "You'd better come in," she said. "You—" she thrust a stubby little finger at Zack "—come with me."

"What's wrong?" Zack asked.

Instead of answering, she pointed at Taylor. "You can take care of Meg and Dianne. They're upstairs. I've got their trays ready in the kitchen." And without another word, she turned and marched down a long hall. With a worried glance at Taylor, Zack followed her, and Taylor hurried after him.

The room at the end of the hall lay shrouded and dim against the afternoon heat; the figure in the bed huddled and tensed beneath the tortured sheets.

"She's sicker than Meg and Dianne," the child said. "And she keeps having that nightmare. Can you help her?"

Cautiously, Zack made his way toward the bed. *Barbara? Is it you? Is it really you?* Yes. Yes, it was. He saw her glazed eyes flutter open as he eased himself onto the side of the bed, and felt the feverish heat of her body as he sat beside her, reaching for and soothing one small, white, clenched fist.

"Zack?" she murmured thickly. "How did you find me?" Her eyes closed again, her breathing deepened. And her hand tightened on his before relaxing in his grasp.

The nightmare was gone, chased away by the firm hand that held hers so protectively. Barbara was safe at last, home at last, loved again—at last. But she had always felt that way when she was with Zack.

Zack. She knew this must be another dream, one conjured up by her fever, but for now she'd take the comfort this dream offered. Later, she would be strong. Later...

Barbara. Zack wanted to cry at the miracle of seeing her again, of holding her, of knowing that, even as vulnerable as she was right now, she didn't shrink from him. But he couldn't—not now. Too much had to be done. And the child was watching—watching him with a curiosity that bordered on obsession.

And Taylor Adams was standing across the room.

"How long has she been like this?" Zack asked.

"Just today," the girl told him. "She was okay when I went to sleep last night."

"And Mrs. Riley? And . . . Dianne?"

"They were real sick, too. But they're better now. I've been taking care of them."

"You're awfully young to have such responsibility."

"I'm six. I'll be in second grade next year."

Zack felt some of the tension leave him. He released Barbara's hand and turned to face the imp who had just conveniently bypassed the fact that she still had to finish the first grade. "We'll get some help in here," he told her. "Do you have a name?"

"Of course." She flounced over to a comfortable blue chair and perched on the edge of it, looking as though she could see into him, or at least wanted to see into him.

"I'm Mickie," she said. "Are you . . . are you my daddy?"

"Who are you? And what the hell are you doing in my house?"

Zack twisted around at the sound of the voice, and Taylor whirled around, too, caught off guard for the first time since Zack had known him.

The woman standing in the doorway would have been stunningly beautiful had her long black hair not been lusterless and tangled, her faded sweatsuit bagged out and wrinkled. But she did command their attention with the utilitarian, no-nonsense, blue steel revolver she held in a utilitarian, no-nonsense, two-handed grip. And she bore little resemblance to the calm and confident author whose photographs he had seen in the Sunday magazine article.

"You," she said to Zack, giving a quick jerk of her head. "Move away from the bed. Mickie, ease over here."

"Good idea," Zack muttered as he stood cautiously and took a step forward.

"Ah, Meg . . ." Mickie began.

"Now!"

The child quirked a grin at Zack but slipped from the chair and walked to the door, passing within inches of Taylor as she did so. Once she reached the door, the woman stepped between her and the men. "Now—" the woman began.

"Mickie," Zack said, "you prepared food for everyone else in the family. Don't you think it's time for you to go to the kitchen and eat something yourself?"

"Not on your life. I wouldn't miss this for the world."

"Mickie." The no-nonsense attitude applied even to the woman's voice. "Go to the front of the house. If I yell, run to the neighbors and call 9-1-1."

Mickie shrugged and grinned at Zack again, but she left the immediate area.

"Now, once more," the woman said. "Who are you? Why are you here? And how did you get in?"

"Mrs. Riley?" Zack asked, although the answer was obvious.

Meg nodded curtly, and Zack realized that her attitude made at least partial confession necessary.

"I'm...I'm Barbara's husband. I was worried about her."

"Her—?" Meg Riley looked at him in stunned disbelief for long seconds before she gave a short gasp of bitter laughter, but she relaxed her firing-range stance and lowered the gun slightly.

"Worried about her?" Her voice failed her, then strengthened. "Now? After the hell she's been through alone? You've got your nerve, Smith. She doesn't need you or your worry. You're about seven years too late—"

"Wait," Zack said, interrupting her. "Smith? Smith is Barbara's maiden name. My name is Gordon. Zack Gordon."

Meg's eyes widened, and again Zack saw the same disbelief, but this time he also saw something else—something that was gone before he could identify it.

"Then who— Zack Gordon?" she asked. "As in Gordon Aviation?"

Zack nodded.

"Oh, my God." Meg's arm dropped to her side, barely holding the forgotten gun, and her voice lowered to little more than a whisper. "She's Barbara Gordon? *That* Barbara Gordon?"

Zack nodded again. The horror in Meg's voice as she obviously remembered the garish newspaper headlines detailing who *that* Barbara Gordon was, was only an echo of his.

Meg glanced toward the bed where Barbara lay deep in her fever-induced sleep, then back at Zack.

"I couldn't find her," he said simply.

"Oh, my God," Meg repeated, whispering now, then falling silent before raising haunted eyes to search his. "I knew she'd been through hell, but not *that*— She never told me...I never dreamed..." She brought her fist to her mouth, then dropped her hand and squared her shoulders. "If you haven't been able to find her for seven years, how did you find her now?"

Zack and Taylor exchanged a long, communicative look. "I was hoping..." He smiled at Meg, acknowledging the futility of his hope. "I was hoping you had contacted my company."

Meg shook her head in reluctant denial. "How could I have?"

"Right. And Barbara—" Zack looked toward the bed. "Barbara asked me how I found her. So she..."

"Wouldn't have," Meg finished for him.

"Right," Zack said again, resigned now. "So that just leaves—"

"Truett," Taylor said grimly.

Meg looked from one man to the other, questions and then comprehension moving across her expressive face. "That horrible man? I thought... Isn't he dead?"

"No," Zack told her. "And the FBI has informed me that he's reported to be back in this country."

"But surely he wouldn't..." she said in little more than a whisper. "He couldn't— Oh! You've got to protect her! You can't let anything else happen to her."

"I won't. He knows he can get to me through her. But she's not the only one in danger. I'm afraid your association with her has put you in jeopardy, too. For your own sake, I want you and your daughters to come with us. My compound is secure. And I hope— I have to believe we'll find Truett soon."

Meg again glanced from Taylor to Zack, then laughed shakily, a nervous gesture with no humor in it. "We're probably going to have a whale of an argument about what you just suggested, but first there's one relevant matter I have to clear up." She hesitated, then straightened her shoulders. "Mickie isn't my child."

Zack looked up to see an overly serious girl peering around the door facing. When she saw him notice her, she ducked out of sight. He smiled at her and her antics before turning serious again. "If she's just an infrequent visitor, she might be safe if we take her to her home. I want to talk with her parents, though, to make sure they understand that if there's any possibility of danger, I will supply body guards."

"No," Meg told him. "I don't think *you* understand." She turned troubled eyes toward Barbara, then visibly made a decision. "Maybe you'd better sit down, Mr. Gordon."

Zack raised a brow in question but remained silent.

"I heard Mickie ask you if you were her father," Meg continued. "That wasn't the off-the-wall question you probably thought it was. You see, Mickie isn't my child, she's Barbara's."

Two

Cocooned. Wrapped up in cotton batting. Smothered. Barbara applied each of those descriptions to the way she felt as she paced through the sterile luxury of a "guest" bedroom in Zack's compound. She had heard him use the term "compound," and it certainly seemed adequate. For this was not a home.

The evening before, she had escaped from the confinement of her room, well enough at last to chafe at her inactivity, and had gone searching for Mickie. She'd found her, asleep in her room two doors down and across a long hallway. The hall stretched away from her in both directions, toward the front of the apartment and the elegant but impersonal rooms she barely remembered Zack carrying her through the night they arrived, and in the other direction, along what seemed to be the length of the building, toward the secret depths of the apartment.

She'd seen Zack's chrome-and-smoked-glass office tower many times since her arrival in Houston, but she'd never

dreamed that he lived in luxurious isolation on the top floor
Safe. Imprisoned.

If she'd had the courage to search for Zack then, would
she have found him? But she hadn't had the courage and she
hadn't searched.

No, this was not a home, she thought again as she looked
around the cream-and-green bedroom he'd carried her to
and left her in. This and all the public rooms she'd seen
seemed to have been designed more for carefully catered
business dinners and receptions than for the curious fingers
of children.

And regardless of what she dimly remembered Zack telling her, she was not a guest; she was a prisoner. And she'd
tell Zack just exactly how she felt about that when—if—she
ever saw him again.

Zack. He hadn't been a dream. And her reaction to that
knowledge scared her as much as the memory of her reaction when she thought he was. She couldn't love Zack Gordon, she couldn't let herself. The cost was too high.

Three days. Had it really been only three days since he'd
swooped down on them, packed them up bag, baggage and
bird cages and moved them all into this . . . this . . . this—

Words failed her as she walked to the French doors and
stood looking out at the lush rooftop garden and land-
scaped pool, open to but protected by the wings of the
sprawling apartment, and past the waist-high brick wall to
the skyline of Houston buildings spread out around them.
True, the compound was safe enough. There were only two
ways in: sixteen floors up by private elevator, or out of the
sky by helicopter.

But Barbara didn't feel "safe." She felt—cocooned,
wrapped up in cotton wool. Smothered.

She felt her lips quirk involuntarily. It was a good thing
Meg was the writer, not she, if her vocabulary was as limited as it seemed to be today.

Her smile faded when she thought of Meg. Oh, Meg was
happy enough here. She swore she could write anywhere she
had access to a computer and to research materials. And
Meg acknowledged that Dianne was content in her new

room with her collection of tropical birds around her and a private tutor instead of the formal confinement of a classroom.

But Meg's attitude had changed toward her. She'd met Meg only a few months after she'd run from Zack, when she had been very confused and very pregnant. Meg had just begun building a respectable reputation for herself as a writer but needed help with her three-year-old invalid daughter. They had become friends, drawing on each other's strength and helping each other through times when those strengths seemed frighteningly insufficient.

But now Meg treated her as though she were some fragile piece of porcelain or crystal.

And Barbara was beginning to feel almost as brittle as either of those two substances.

And Zack? He'd dumped her in this luxurious prison and then absented himself to some other part of it, leaving her to the tender mercies of a doctor and a private-duty nurse.

A nurse, for God's sake! When all she had was the flu, and when all she wanted was—

Was what?

To make the last seven years never to have happened?

To go back to the innocent she had been when she'd fallen in love with Zachary Gordon?

But that would mean no Mickie.

And Mickie. Precocious, irreverent Mickie had been both her sentence in hell and her hope of heaven, and was now the only constant in Barbara's life.

"Mom!" that constant said, bursting through the doorway and brandishing a hairbrush. "I want a French braid."

Barbara's lips twitched, but she kept herself from laughing.

"What brought about this desire?" she asked.

"Well, Dianne has one. And that nurse of yours— Is she coming back?"

Barbara took the brush from Mickie and led her to the dressing table. "No, I don't need her anymore."

"Well, that's good," Mickie said as she hopped up onto the chair. "I mean, that you don't need her, not that she's gone. She was neat."

"Yes," Barbara admitted, running the brush through her daughter's curls. "She was."

"But she did Dianne's hair and didn't stay long enough to do mine."

Barbara grinned, put down the brush and stretched one of Mickie's copper-colored curls to its inconsequential length. "Look at that, Mickie."

"So?"

"So... the nurse would have had to stay here an awfully long time to braid this hair."

"Oh." Mickie's mouth turned down and her lower lip thrust out as she studied the problem. "Maybe..." she offered. "Maybe you could learn to do it by the time I get it to grow long enough?"

"It's a deal," Barbara told her.

"Mom?" Mickie squirmed around and patted the chair seat beside her. Barbara smiled and accepted the well-known invitation, scooping Mickie onto her lap as she sat in the chair.

"What is it, pumpkin?"

"*Don't* call me that."

"Oops, sorry. I forgot you don't like it anymore." The nickname was, in fact, one that Mickie had dreamed up and insisted on being called for months after she saw Barbara baking a pumpkin pie. But Mickie's attitude had turned serious, too serious for easy bantering. Barbara gave Mickie a comforting squeeze. "What is it, darling?"

"Is Zack—?" Mickie twisted in Barbara's arms so she could look up at her face. "Is Zack my daddy?"

Barbara felt her hard-earned strength drain from her. Mickie's questions about her father were inevitable, had been inevitable even without the appearance of Zachary Gordon in her young life. Barbara had known that one day she would have to answer them—but not so soon! Not with Mickie looking at her with so much love... and so much trust... and so much... innocence.

"What makes you..." Barbara swallowed once, twice. *Zack would be asking the same question!* That knowledge tightened around her heart. "What makes you ask that question, Mickie?" she managed to say.

"Because of your dream." Mickie's little hand reached for Barbara's. "The really bad one you have. You know."

Barbara gripped her daughter's hand. "Yes, I know. I just didn't know you did."

Mickie shook her head. "Of course I know, Mom. And when you have this dream, sometimes you talk."

"No," Barbara whispered. *What did she say? What had her daughter heard?*

"And when you talk, you always ask for someone named Zack. That's why I opened the door for him the other day. He said his name was Zack. You don't think I'd let strangers in the house, do you? So...is he my daddy?"

"Mickie, I..." She wrapped her arms around her daughter and held her close, rocking gently. "Mr. Gordon is a very nice man and I—" She felt tears closing her throat and brimming in her eyes and willed them not to fall. "You are *my* daughter, Mickie. I love you very much, and that's all I can tell you now. Please trust me. And please, please love me even though I can't answer your question."

Mickie gave an exasperated sigh. "Of course I love you. Is this one of those grown-up things I'll understand later?"

"Oh, I hope so, baby. I really hope so."

There would be no good time to talk with Zack. Barbara knew that as surely as she knew she must talk with him. As surely as she knew she must leave. As surely as she knew she must never let him know she— She what? Loved him? Love was a luxury she couldn't afford, a curse that could damn both her and Zack and, ultimately, Mickie.

Talk, Barbara reminded herself the next morning when she heard the sounds of Mickie's and Dianne's young voices mingled with Zack's deep baritone drifting through the open French doors into her room. *Talk. Before you lose what nerve you have.*

She walked to the doors and looked out into the clear
morning light. Mickie and Dianne were in the pool, acting
like the water babies they had been trained to be almost since
birth, because in the buoyancy of the water, Dianne could
move and play as gracefully as one day, thanks to the skill
of the surgeons at Children's Medical Hospital, she would
be able to move on dry land.

Dressed in plain black swim trunks, modest she supposed by today's standards and probably in deference to the
children, Zack knelt beside the ledge of the pool, talking to
the girls. He had obviously been in the pool. His hair, dripping wet, seemed almost black slicked back from his face,
while rivulets of water kissed him slowly as they made their
way down his still sleek body. Zack had once told her his
grandmother was part Cheyenne, which helped explain his
lack of abundant body hair—but he did have a light dusting of dark hair on his tautly muscled chest, legs and fore-
arms, accented now by the water caressing him. As she once
had. As she...

Talk! she urged herself.

As she watched, Mickie swam to him. Zack extended his
arm to the child, and in an apparently effortless motion
pulled her from the pool to stand beside him. After an ab-
breviated conference, they both turned to face the pool,
Zack demonstrating a diving pose while Mickie studied,
then copied the pose. Zack executed a shallow dive, all grace
in motion, then watched as Mickie copied the dive.

And Barbara felt tears welling in her eyes and a fist the
size of the Houston skyline bruising her heart. *Stop it!* she
told herself. *Now! Before we all get hurt.* But even as she
stepped from the cool shade of her room into the garden,
she knew it was too late. At least for her. The pain had already begun. Or maybe it had never stopped.

"Mickie," she called.

Mickie didn't seem to hear her, but Zack did. Almost as
though he had been waiting for her arrival, he turned in the
pool, swam to the side, and levered himself out.

Mickie saw her then, turning and waving. "Hi, Mom. Are
you coming in? Did you see the great dive Zack taught me?

I bet it'll give me a head start on anybody in a race. I can't believe how far out in the lap it puts me.''

Zack stood and slipped into a thigh-length, terry-cloth robe. Trapped in his eyes, Barbara barely heard her daughter's joyful words, although she was all too aware of the joy. *Too late*, she thought. *It's too late*.

"That's wonderful, Mickie," she managed to say. "And good morning, Dianne. Now, if you two dolphins in training can tear yourselves away from the pool, Meg is waiting breakfast for you."

Mickie grimaced but dog-paddled to the side of the pool. Once out, she gave a hand to Dianne, always solicitous of the older girl and always careful not to let Dianne know. "Are you coming, Mom?"

Barbara shook her head, and Mickie turned hopefully. "Are you, Zack?"

Zack smiled but shook his head, too. "Not today, pumpkin. Your mom and I have to talk."

Pumpkin? Barbara cut a quick glance at her daughter, but Mickie only raised her brows in a too innocent Orphan Annie impression and shrugged her shoulders before taking Dianne's arm and hurrying the older girl into the penthouse.

"You'll want to get dressed," Barbara said, hoping Zack wouldn't hear the desperation in her voice.

"I would," he admitted, "if I didn't have the feeling that if I let you out of my sight, you'll disappear again, and I can't let that happen." He lifted one arm toward her, then shifted position and gestured toward chairs and a round table beside a leafy, towering vine growing on a latticed trellis. "Are you sure you don't want any breakfast?" he asked.

Barbara shook her head. "This isn't going to be a social occasion," she said around the tightness in her throat, but when he walked to the chairs and sat, she followed. "Zack..."

A carafe of coffee waited on the table. Zack poured two cups, set one at a place across the table from his, and sat sipping from the other, waiting. He wasn't as calm as he wanted her to think, Barbara realized as she saw the tiny twitch at the right side of his finely sculpted mouth. He was, in fact, furious. With her? Or with the situation? It didn't matter, she acknowledged. She needed his anger. Anger was so much easier to bear than pain.

She sat and lifted the cup to her lips, barely tasting the fragrant brew before replacing the cup in its saucer. "Zack, I... Thank you for taking care of us while I was ill. I'm sorry to have imposed on you. We'll return to Meg's house this afternoon—"

"Running away again, Barbara?" he asked, and she saw the twitch deepen. "How old is Mickie?"

He always could cut right to the heart of an issue. "Six." She stood and gathered her dignity. "Thank you for your hospitality—"

"Sit down!"

Startled, she could only stare at him. Zack had never raised his voice to her.

He looked up at her, his dark eyes haunted. "I didn't find you, Barbara. Someone called my security office and told us where you were. Someone who apparently wanted me to know about you and Mickie. It wasn't you—"

Barbara dragged her head from one side to the other in mute denial.

"And it wasn't Meg. Who else do you suppose would have any interest in my knowing the whereabouts of the woman who left me seven years ago and who now has a six-year-old daughter?"

The strength drained from her legs and she sank onto the chair. "No," she whimpered.

Zack reached across the table and, after a moment's hesitation, took her hands in his. "I know you're afraid. You have every right to be. I know I failed you before, but I swear on everything I hold holy that I will protect you this time. He won't get you again."

"Why now?" she whispered.

"I don't know." He shook his head. "That's not entirely true. I suspect the cause. I just don't understand the reasoning. We're developing a major modification in the jet engine, one that drastically cuts fuel consumption while boosting efficiency. The defense department is interested—the entire industry is interested—but I fail to see any profit for Truett."

"He doesn't need a reason. He's beyond needing a reason," she said in a flat voice. "But I'm not a part of your life anymore. He won't use me again." She pulled her hands from Zack's, feeling the tingle of loss as she clenched her hands into fists. "I'm leaving, Zack. You can't stop me."

"The hell I can't!" Zack erupted from his chair and paced to the pool and back. He stood over her, radiating anger he barely controlled—anger and another emotion Barbara was very much afraid she recognized. With visible effort, he straightened away from her. "If you won't think about yourself, think about Mickie. You know what perversity Truett is capable of." Barbara felt herself shrinking back into the chair as Zack's words tore at her carefully erected barriers. "Think what he could do if he got his hands on my daughter."

"Stop it!"

Barbara pushed out of her chair and stood before him, trembling. "Stop it," she whispered.

"Barbara, I'm sorry." Zack dropped a hand onto her shoulder. "God, I'm sorry. I wouldn't hurt you for the world, but you can't put yourself or Mickie in danger."

Barbara stepped away from his touch and hugged her arms around herself, trembling. God, she couldn't stop trembling.

"I understand why you left," Zack said, his voice old, tired. "I can even accept why you never wanted to see me again. What I can't understand is why you didn't tell me about Mickie. How you could have left me while you were carrying our child. After our plans, our hopes, our dreams, how could you have denied me knowledge of, the companionship of—the *love* of my daughter—"

"Zack." Her voice soft but firm, she silenced him. She felt one tear sliding from the corner of her eye and dared it to fall. She never cried. She couldn't cry now. She wouldn't. "I wasn't pregnant when I met you in Charleston. I didn't know I was pregnant when I left."

She watched him blanch as though struck, his muscles tighten as though readying for fight, and finally, his eyes dull against a pain she knew too well.

"So you see," she continued softly, "he has no use for either of us. To him, I'm simply a divorced woman, and Mickie is—Mickie is my illegitimate child."

Zack shuddered once, then became the Zachary Gordon she had once seen in a board room, a Zachary Gordon she was just a little afraid of.

"Did you really think I'd divorce you without talking with you, without seeing for myself that you meant what you said in that semicoherent note, without...without learning if there was anything I could do to save our marriage?"

"Zack, it's been seven years."

"I know. Believe me, I know." He shook off the weakness those words seemed to have caused him. "So *you* see," he said with a frightening calm, "you are still my wife and, at least in the eyes of the law, Mickie *is* my child.

"Make yourself comfortable, Barbara, because you are going to be here as long as I think it's necessary for your safety to keep you here. But I'll do my best not to bother you or...or your daughter any more than is absolutely necessary."

Zack sat in the deep leather chair in his office a floor below the penthouse. A large, strangely marked, gray-striped cat crouched on the floor beside his feet, not purring, as though sharing the thick tension in the room. Zack had been there all day, stopping only to dress when he'd left Barbara; not to eat, not to work. He had warned his staff not to disturb him. And he had sat in the chair, watching but not seeing as the clear brightness of the morning changed to the muggy oppression of the afternoon, to the gaudy display of sunset, to the velvet haze of twilight.

He sat alone with the silent cat, now in the dark, with only the lights of the city spread out around him to cast any illumination on the harsh, emotionless planes of his face.

A Scotch bottle sat on the table beside him, as did one heavy, cut-crystal tumbler. Both were empty, as empty as his soul felt, but the Scotch had not dulled his memories.

Truett had taken Barbara from a sidewalk in downtown Atlanta. She and Zack had been in Charleston, South Carolina, the night before, in a beautifully maintained nineteenth-century home owned by a friend of Zack's, a home he and Barbara were considering buying. They'd been taking a belated honeymoon—both his and her work had kept them from taking one a few months ago. They'd had the house to themselves—Zack's friend was still in Europe, where Zack had gone for a business trip that had stretched from one week, to two, to three.

They'd never been separated so much as a night before, but Barbara hadn't been able to get away from her project long enough to join him in Hanover, Germany. She had met him at the Charleston house, and they had fallen on each other like recently escaped prisoners. Only later were they able to laugh at their haste and the unseemly use they had made of the hallway's Oriental rug. Then they'd taken champagne, fruit and cheese to the master bedroom and picnicked in the massive four-poster.

"Let's make a baby," Zack whispered, nuzzling the sensitive spot just behind Barbara's right ear. "I know we talked about waiting, but let's do it now. A little girl that looks just like you."

Barbara turned in his arms, moaning and laughing at the same time. "Or a little boy that looks like you. You don't think God would— Oh, yes! Zack... Is this something new you've learned?"

"Hush, woman, I'm making love to my wife."

"And very well. I just thought you might like some constructive criticism. Like this," she said, moving against him.

"I see what you mean." Zack took her lead and let her push him back into the feather mattress. "Woman, what are you doing to me?"

"Just helping," she said, looking down at him, love and mischief and unadulterated passion in her eyes. "With the baby, I mean."

"Oh, yes." Talking was becoming almost impossible. *"The baby. What were you saying about God—and the baby?"*

"Just...just—" she gasped as he touched her. Her mouth opened in surprise, then twisted in a triumphant smile, but she wasn't yet ready to surrender completely to the passion. *"Just that—you don't think he would get our orders mixed up do you? I mean, give us a little girl that looked like you. God wouldn't play that kind of joke on us, would he?"*

"No," Zack told her, rolling so that she was beneath him, and the feather mattress billowed up around them. *"At least, I don't think so. Maybe we'd better hurry and find out—"*

"Zack?"

Taylor Adams's voice invaded Zack's memories. He turned in the darkness and glared at the outline of the man standing in the light spilling through the open door. Taylor's hand moved over the wall, and light filled the room. He walked across the room and stood in front of Zack. "Is there anything I can do?"

Anesthetize me, drug me, knock me over the head and put me out of my misery? Zack wondered what Taylor would say if he voiced any of those thoughts. Probably nothing. And he wondered what Taylor would say if he ordered him to kill a man.

Thank God, you were not the one to have to kill someone.

But he'd wanted to. He still wanted to. The police had killed two men in the shoot-out when they'd found Barbara. Not Truett. He'd escaped. Would killing him be enough? Would Zack finally be rid of the pain and the deep sense of failure?

Thank God, you were not the one to have to kill someone. I don't think I could live with myself if you had been brought to that because of me.

"Zack? Is there anything I can do."

Zack reached for the bottle of Scotch and remembered it was empty. For a moment he considered asking Taylor to get him another and then he pushed away that impulse. His

thoughts were too uncontrolled as it was. If he couldn't
drink himself into oblivion, he needed to be able to think
clearly. *Had* they made a baby that one night? Or was this
something else Truett had stolen from him?

"I want a complete medical profile on Truett," he said.
"Blood type, history, childhood illnesses, DNA if it's available. And I want him found. Hire whoever you need. I want
him found *now*."

Barbara was asleep when Zack looked in on her, curled up
on her side with the sheet pulled up under her chin. Her hair
was the color of warm honey. Once she had slept with it
loose and free on his pillow. Now her hair was braided, and
even the braid was under the sheet. She was all restrained,
tidy and tucked in. There was little sign of the Barbara he
had known. And how could there be? He wanted to go to
the bed and gather her in his arms, but he knew he couldn't
do that.

"I love you," he whispered to the sleeping woman. "I
never stopped loving you, not once in all the long, lonely
years you've been hiding."

Did she hate him? Zack didn't think so, but he couldn't
be sure. God knew, she had reason to. But she had loved
him once. And at least for now, she needed him. Maybe that
would be enough for them to begin to rebuild their marriage. And maybe there would be enough time for him to
show her that he could keep her safe, that she needed him—
and not just for her safety—as much as he needed her.

And the child? Mickie. Precocious, irreverent Mickie.
The love of Barbara's life. How did he feel about Mickie
now?

Maybe the whiskey had had some effect on him, Zack
acknowledged bitterly. Sober, he would never have tears on
his cheeks. Clenching his hands into fists, choking back the
tears, the memories and the pain, he looked again at Barbara. Could she love him again? And he—knowing that
loving her would mean never hurting her or her daughter—
could he truly love her?

"I'll try," he whispered into the darkness, promising her—promising himself—knowing that he never again wanted the pain of living without her but not sure he could survive the pain of living with her. "I swear I will try."

Three

———

Barbara didn't know what had awakened her, or how long Zack had been standing just inside her bedroom doorway. He stood there for several long moments, very still, very quiet, his face hidden in shadows as she knew hers must be, and then he left.

She allowed herself the luxury of one deep, ragged breath, and rolled onto her back, staring at the ceiling.

Once, she had dreamed of Zack finding her, holding her in his arms, telling her that he loved her, that nothing that had happened or would happen could change that, that he would protect her and keep her—keep them both—safe.

Once, she had dreamed that he had convinced her her exile was unnecessary.

But that had been only in her dreams. Awake, she knew none of those dreams could ever be.

And that had been before Mickie.

She'd known he was in Houston, of course—there was no way she wouldn't have kept track of his life, or his career—and had argued with Meg about her move. But how could

she argue against moving Dianne closer to the medical fa
cilities and specialists in Houston so that at last they coul
complete the surgeries made necessary by Dianne's man
birth defects? She'd needed hip and leg operations to en
able her to walk properly. And how much danger, she ha
rationalized, would there be of a housekeeper being broug
to his attention? To anyone's attention?

To Wilson Truett's attention?

She fought the chill that shuddered through her; foug
her body's instinctive need to curl protectively into itself.

He wouldn't use her again. She was of no further value t
him. Unless he thought she was of value to Zack.

And Mickie? She caught the moan in her throat and hel
it back. She had been so careful. She had never lied abou
Mickie being her child, but with Meg's help she had let th
outside world think Mickie was Meg's child, too. *Had* True
found out about her? *When* had he found out about her
And if he knew about Mickie, did he also realize there wa
every possibility that *he* was her biological father?

That wouldn't have mattered to him. Barbara knew tha
with a certainty. Family meant nothing to him. She ha
learned that during the hours she had been forced to liste
to the words of hate spewing from his warped and twiste
mind. Hate for Zack, who had done nothing but be th
loved son of the man Truett's widowed mother had ma
ried.

No. She had been of no further use to Truett, and Mick
would have been of no use whatsoever. Until Zack ha
swooped down on them, gathered them up, and given h
stepbrother a reason and an avenue for venting his hatred

He doesn't need a reason. He's beyond needing a reaso

Barbara shivered again, but sat up and threw off th
sheet. She knew that even sleep would not be safe for her t
rest of the night.

Without turning on the light, she rummaged through th
unfamiliar chest and closet until she found her bathing su
and slipped it on. Physical exhaustion was the only thi
that would let her sleep, and the pool seemed to be the on

place to seek that exhaustion without awakening the rest of the household.

She swam like someone possessed. Lap after lap, back and forth, caught in silhouette of the pool's underwater lighting. Zack watched her from his post near the small table where he had been sitting when she'd emerged from her bedroom, tossed her robe and towel onto a nearby chaise and dived cleanly and competently into the pool.

He ought to leave. He'd known that when she'd first dived into the water. He ought to give her the solitude and privacy she so obviously wanted. But after several minutes, he knew he couldn't leave her alone.

All he wanted to do was dive in after her and stop her from her punishing exercise. But he couldn't do that, either; he knew what demons drove her. And holding her in his arms, no matter how much that would comfort him, wouldn't make her demons go away.

So he watched, silent and still, until finally she began to tire. At last she attempted to heave herself out of the pool. And slipped. And again she tried. And slipped.

Unable to stand silent any longer, Zack strode to the edge of the pool and knelt beside her. She looked up, her hazel eyes wide, vulnerable, and yet somehow resigned to whatever fate decided to hurl at her.

He lifted her from the pool and, when her legs failed to support her, held her while he wrapped her heavy terry-cloth robe around her and bundled her dripping braid in the towel. She stiffened when he lifted her into his arms but relaxed, or collapsed, against him as he carried her into her room, still looking up at him, her eyes pleading with him. But for what, he had no idea.

He lowered her onto her bed, not wanting to let her go but knowing he had to, and for endless moments as he looked into her eyes his body and his heart demanded that he lean forward, that he claim at least a kiss for all that had been taken from them seven years before. Barely aware of his actions, he actually did lean forward, but as he did so, he heard her stifled sob and felt her body tense.

Holding himself still, silently and fluently he cursed himself, Truett, the world in general, and even, for a moment, God. Then, with a tenderness he was far from feeling, he drew Barbara's robe more securely closed and left the room.

She actually slept. Dreamlessly. Until just before dawn. Then the dream slipped in, capturing her.

Let's make a baby.

I love you, Barbara.

I'll always love you.

With a whimper, she awoke, shivering and chilled from her damp hair and suit. She showered and shampooed, washing away the memories and her weakness of the night before, trying to wash away her dreams. Then, dressed in her customary slacks and tailored cotton shirt, her hair neatly braided, she prepared herself to face Zack once again over the breakfast table.

The first videotape arrived at ten that morning. Seated at his desk in the midst of the familiar insanity of his office, Zack had almost convinced himself he had imagined the danger surrounding him, surrounding Barbara.

And he had almost convinced himself that even if the danger were real, he was prepared to confront it.

But he wasn't prepared for the sight of Taylor Adams standing in his office doorway, holding a black, plastic videocassette case and looking grim.

Zack stared at the case, at the pale green mailer he knew it had been wrapped in, not yet believing as he felt the chill of fear, new and remembered, slither through him.

"It came by courier," Adams told him. "To my attention. The messenger company noted only that it was dropped off at a pickup site with a cash payment."

"You watched it?" Zack asked, but the question was rhetorical. Of course Taylor had watched it. And who else?

Adams nodded and walked across the room to Zack' own television and videocassette recorder and inserted the tape.

With a sick fascination that he recognized all too easily, Zack faced the television screen and watched the seemingly innocent images. A pleasant, tree-lined street in an affluent subdivision; a flagstone sidewalk leading up to a sprawling stone house; a subcompact car pulling up to the curb and a gum-popping, gangly teenage boy walking up to the door with a small paper bag in his hand; Barbara opening the door, taking the package, handing the boy what appeared to be payment.

"Damn it, Zack. This footage was shot after we had security in place for her. That's the drugstore delivery Wilcox told us about. There to the right, you can see our van—"

Zack waved him to silence.

Wilson Truett's hideous little films had never contained just one scene.

Zack watched the scene fade out in a manner once made possible only by an editing room—which was how the FBI caught Wilson—but now possible for anyone with two VCR's and a video camera, and then his stepbrother's trademark appeared. From some old movie or action-adventure movie serial, Wilson had captured a clock face with the hands moving rapidly around it, denoting the passage of time, eventually disappearing as the image of the stone house faded in.

The front door opened, and Barbara, looking as though she were already succumbing to the flu that had later debilitated her, walked out onto the sidewalk. Stooping, she picked up a newspaper, then straightened and looked around, her head slightly cocked as though listening, or searching.

Zack saw her frown slightly as she looked toward his surveillance van, then shake her head as though in quick and incredulous denial before turning and walking slowly back into the house.

Once again the clock face appeared, spinning on in its mad race, and then static filled the television screen.

Zack slumped back into his desk chair. The tension still thrummed through him, but for now the horror was bearable. "Leave that with me," he told Adams. "And bring the next one to me without watching it."

"Zack—"

"I mean it, Taylor," Zack said, pushing up out of his chair. "No one watches those tapes but me. No one!"

"You think there will be more?"

Zack turned back toward the now blank television screen. "I used to think there was no such thing as evil," he said slowly and carefully. "Perhaps there could be an absence of good, or a selfish and therefore dangerous-to-others way of looking at the world. But now I'm sure that *evil* exists—my stepbrother has taught me that—and I'm equally sure that there will be more tapes. He's not through with us yet."

"I know you don't want to hear this," Taylor said, equally slowly, equally carefully, "but I don't think he could have done this alone. You have to consider the danger you might be putting yourself in. You have to consider who his accomplice might be."

Zack grew very still, very quiet as he absorbed Taylor's accusations. "You can't believe that Barbara would align herself with Wilson against me. My God, haven't you heard what I've told you about how he—what he put her through?"

"I can't afford to trust her, Zack, not when your safety is at stake. And neither can you. I know you said she was his prisoner, but we've all heard of the Stockholm syndrome, where the prisoner—"

"Grows to love the captor?" Zack interrupted, derision twisting his face and thickening his voice.

"Yes," Taylor persisted. "And there's the child. What kind of hold does he have over her because of the child? Her showing up, here, at this time, is either coincidence or conspiracy—"

"I don't know what happened in your past to make you so cynical about women," Zack said, interrupting him, knowing that Taylor must be wondering about Mickie's parentage but unwilling to hear him voice those suspicions. "And I couldn't have worked with you this long without realizing that something must have." He held up a hand to silence Taylor's denial. "But I do know that Barbara was no more responsible for what happened to you than she is for what's happening now."

"I don't believe in coincidence, not of this magnitude," Taylor said, remaining silent about his past but not letting go of the skepticism in his voice. "And you pay me very well to dig out and defend you against conspiracy."

"Then do so. But stop thinking of Barbara as part of it, so you can discover who really is. I don't want to hear any more accusations against her. And you're not to say one word to her about your suspicions, or about this tape. I won't have her subjected to any more fear than she already is. Is that clear?"

Taylor ejected the cassette from the machine and walked to Zack's desk. He held out the tape, standing there until Zack took it from him. "Yes," he said softly. "Very clear. I only wish your thinking was half as clear."

"Barbara?"

Barbara looked up from the magazine at which she had been staring blankly and scrambled from the chaise longue in her room.

"Meg!" she said with genuine joy. "I missed you at breakfast this morning. I was only waiting until after your work hours to come searching for you. Come in. *Please* come in."

Meg smiled hesitantly as she entered the room. "Are you sure? I'm not . . . I'm not interrupting anything—not disturbing you, am I?"

What was this? Meg? Unsure of her welcome after all they had been through together? Quickly Barbara crossed the room and took Meg's arm, leading her to the chaise.

"You're kidding, right?" Barbara asked with an incredulous laugh as she moved her free arm in a broad, sweeping gesture toward the immaculate room and the one magazine. "Of course, I've let my housework get horribly out of control, and my reading is piling up . . ."

Meg's smile had faded. Barbara paused in her futile attempt at humor. She sank onto the chaise and tugged on Meg's arm until she sat beside her.

"What's wrong?" Barbara asked. "Dianne?" When Meg remained silent, she pushed on. "Your work? The strange surroundings? Meg, you told me everything was all right. Have I—? Can I—?"

Meg's continued silence and the hesitation and regret Barbara saw in her eyes frightened her. "We've been friends too long for you not to tell me what's wrong," she said, trying to keep that fear from her voice. Meg's friendship had been a constant in her life for too long; she couldn't lose that friendship now.

"I..." Meg took Barbara's hand in a tight grasp. "Have we?" she asked. "Been friends? Really?"

"Of course," Barbara answered, troubled by the question, by Meg's need to ask it. "We've been there for each other since the day you finally decided to take a chance and hire me—through Dianne's surgeries and Mickie's tonsillectomy—through that horrible contract foul-up with your last publisher and your award ceremony last year."

"But you didn't— Why didn't you trust me enough to tell me who you really were?"

Now Barbara was the one who grasped Meg's hand. "Would it really have made a difference?"

Meg drew in a sharp, shuddering breath, and Barbara saw the glimmer of moisture in her eyes before Meg caught her in a tight hug. "I would never have betrayed that trust, Barbara. I would never—ever—have hurt you."

"Do you think I don't know that?" Barbara asked, returning Meg's hug and feeling the slight tremor that ran through her friend's body.

"I don't know much of anything anymore," Meg said, sniffling once and beginning to pull away.

"Mom!" The door burst open and Mickie marched in with Dianne following. "Oh, there you are, Meg. Dianne couldn't find you." Mickie's eyes narrowed as she studied the two women. "Are you all right?"

Meg gave a short laugh and rose to her feet. "Of course I'm all right," she said. "Am I ever not?"

Was Meg all right? Barbara pondered that question long after Meg had let the girls lead her off for a round of computer games. Or was this latest visit just another step in Meg's changing attitude toward her—a step in the direction of a pity she would not tolerate brought on by a past she could no longer hide?

In the early years of her exile, Barbara had told herself that the worst thing that could happen to her would be never to see Zack again, never to laugh with him, to love with him, to *be* with him.

Now, less than a week after he had found her, she knew better.

The worst thing that could happen was happening.

She was on the edge of his life, but not with him. She was married to him, but not his wife. She was in his home, but as a stranger.

And she couldn't leave.

Her choices were none. Because to leave meant to risk destroying the child who now was her life.

She saw Zack at meals, polite interludes where they all gathered—to all appearances, an extended family but with the only spontaneity present being that of the young girls, Mickie and Dianne.

And she occasionally saw Zack at other times, equally polite interludes where each was careful not to rake up old memories, old wounds, old emotions, and, for her, old hungers.

But Zack was obviously holding *himself* aloof, or at least distant, from both her and Mickie. He had not again forced a confrontation with her. She no longer told herself she had to talk with him.

After all, what was there left to say? She had run from him; he had found her. She had a child he hadn't known about—a child conceived no earlier than a June night in Charleston a lifetime ago and no later than the night before she was rescued.

She couldn't tell him any of the things that once he would have wanted to hear, that once she would have wanted to say. And she couldn't tell him what she herself didn't know, couldn't know—refused to know.

And she was all alone. Zack's employees were efficient and polite, almost to a fault, but in their actions she saw cynicism and a barely veiled distrust—of her. It didn't extend to Mickie, thank God, or to Meg or Dianne. And would never have been shown to the beloved young wife of Zack Gordon she had once been.

But perhaps that was for the best. Barbara had learned long ago that for some people safety lay in having no emotional ties. Without trust, she was in no danger of building friendships she would have to abandon.

The second tape arrived four days after the first, delivered anonymously by a different messenger company but in the same type of pale green envelope Zack had learned long ago to hate—or to fear.

Taylor brought it directly to his office without opening it, but there he insisted on being the one to break the seal, to lift out the tape, to insert it in the machine.

"Leave," Zack said, tight-lipped, holding out his hand for the remote control.

"But Zack—"

"Leave the room, I said." Zack shook his head, forcing himself to relax, forcing himself to moderate his voice, his actions, his dread of what might be on this missal from hell. "But don't go far. I'll want you back in here in a few minutes."

Taylor studied him quietly but eventually handed him the remote control. "I'll be in your outer office," he said.

Zack nodded abruptly and waited until his chief of security closed the door behind him before he walked around his desk, leaned against it, and studied the still blank television. For a full minute he held the remote poised, then, drawing in a breath, pushed the Play button.

He recognized the man who had been his photographer pull his car to the curb across the street and down a short

distance from Meg Riley's house. A few interminable minutes later, after viewing nothing but the front of the house
and the gently moving leaves on the oaks along the sidewalk, he watched the station wagon pull out of Meg's
driveway with Barbara at the wheel, disappearing down the
street with the photographer's car following her.

Fade-out to the racing clock. Fade-in to Barbara returning to the house with a station wagon full of children, all
girls, who scattered to various houses along the street, leaving Barbara, Mickie and Dianne alone in the driveway.

Pan back to the photographer, once again in place, as he
captured that scene for Zack eventually to see, to act upon.

Once again the racing clock filled the screen. Zack wanted
to turn the damn thing off, but he couldn't—not until he
was sure this was all Truett's twisted mind had in store for
him. Only when static filled the screen did he stop the tape
and start rewinding it while he forced himself to go to his
office door.

Coincidence? Or conspiracy? Or just damn good planning on the part of a sick and devious mind? Zack suspected the latter, but he knew that Taylor Adams's
unreasonable suspicions were about to be strongly rein-
forced by the tape that Zack had no true option but to show
him.

Barbara leaned against the chest-high wall of the roof
garden and watched the lights of downtown Houston glittering in the distance.

Mickie was in bed, at last asleep. Zack—Zack had long
ago disappeared into wherever it was he took himself to
avoid being with her or her daughter. Barbara was alone.
But this was no luxury for her. With nothing to occupy her
time or her hands, her agile and creative mind had far too
much unstructured freedom.

What did one do in a luxurious nest, haven, prison such
as Zack's penthouse? Barbara had wondered that more than
once as the days dragged on, as the edge of panic dulled.

Not visit with Meg. They hadn't really talked since that
unsettling visit in Barbara's room. Besides, Meg was em-

broiled in a problem plot and a rapidly approaching deadline.

Not visit with Mickie, at least not during the day, because she and Dianne were closeted with their tutor and makeup work.

Not care for the nest, as she had done for the past seven years. Zack's more than efficient staff saw adequately and competently to every housekeeping need.

Not even care for her own portion of the nest, she had learned when she'd returned to her room that first morning she had ventured out to breakfast. The bed had been made, the bathroom neatened, the towels replaced.

Not anything, she realized. Not—

"Barbara."

She clutched at the cool brick of the wall as Zack's soft, low voice shattered her thoughts.

"Barbara?"

She turned slowly, not ready to face him again without the buffer of other people between them but knowing that she must. He looked harassed—haggard almost—as though he wasn't sleeping, worse, much worse than he had looked earlier that day. He had dressed for business, as he always did during the week, but sometime during the day he had pulled off his tie and rolled up his cuffs. His hair, almost black in the dim light of the roof garden and slightly longer than his corporate image would lead one to expect, had lost the just-from-the-barber look he so easily maintained, and his cheeks were shadowed with his evening beard. And his eyes... Oh, Lord, his eyes were weary beyond belief, haunted almost, as she had seen them once before, as she had sworn she would never see them again.

"What's wrong?" she asked, stopping herself as she realized she was about to reach for him.

A ghost of a smile flitted across his face and then just as quickly disappeared. "I was about to ask you the same thing. You looked so...so pensive. Is there something you need? Anything I can get for you?"

A new past? she wondered, her thoughts flying free and unfettered only for the space of a heartbeat. A future?

"No. Thank you," she said, forcing herself to lean back against the wall. "You've been more than thoughtful in seeing to our needs. Meg is delighted with the computer you've given her to use, and Mickie and Dianne seem quite comfortable with Mr. Jameson as a tutor."

"And you? What do *you* want, Barbara?"

For you to wrap me in your arms and hold me safe and comforted. To let me, just for a little while, not be strong, not be determined, not be so terribly, irrevocably alone. But she couldn't tell him that. If he hadn't caught her at such a weak moment, she wouldn't even have allowed herself to think it.

"Actually," she said, drawing a deep breath, "I feel almost guilty for saying this, because you've provided so carefully for us—I need something to *do*."

She thought a shadow crossed his face, but it was gone so quickly she thought she must have imagined it, until he spoke.

"Are you sure you're strong enough to do anything? Perhaps you should rest a few more days."

"Zack, I had the flu, not some life-threatening disease. All of us had the flu, and everyone else is working now."

"What do you...?" His hesitation was slight, but so unexpected it seemed to shout at her although he kept his voice low. "What do you think might interest you?"

"I don't know," she said honestly, shrugging and motioning toward the penthouse. "Everything here is so smoothly run, there's no need for my interference."

"But you don't really want to manage the household, do you?"

"No. I..."

"Perhaps something with your past training?"

"Oh, Zack. Do you think so? Surely there's some way I can be of help, either to you or to the company."

She wondered at his deep sigh, at the way he closed his eyes briefly before looking past her, not at her. "Have you kept up with the industry?"

"Oh," she said quietly. That question said it all. He doubted her abilities. And he was right to do so. "No. I'm

afraid I haven't, except for information that filtered down
to the general public.''

"Then—" He shook his head, but once again looked at
her. "Why don't I have Jamie—Mr. Jameson, to the girls—
go through the company library and start bringing you some
material to help you catch up on what's been happening in
the past few years.''

Not "Why don't I take you down to the company library
and let you dig around to your heart's content the way you
once did?" But Barbara sensed that Zack felt he had made
a major concession to her. Why? Surely she would be as safe
in his building as she was in his penthouse. Surely he didn'
think she'd run away again, not with her daughter at risk.

"Thank you," she said. "That would be... I— Thanks.'
Should she ask him, remind him again of her question that
he had so neatly sidestepped? Once she would have. Had she
forfeited the right? Did it matter? "Now," she said quietly
"what's—?"

A scream ripped through the night air, paralyzing Bar
bara and holding Zack immobile for no more than a second.

"Dianne," Barbara whispered, recognizing the continu-
ing cries, and turning, starting to run at the same instant
Zack grabbed her arm, stopping her.

"Nightmare?" he asked tersely.

"Never."

"Wait here," he demanded before leaving on a dead run
toward the direction of Dianne's bedroom.

"No way," she murmured, taking out after him, only
gaining on him when he slowed at a control panel to hit a
switch and yell into it, "Get up here. Now!"

Mickie and Meg had reached the room before them. Zack
shouldered his way into Dianne's room and flipped the light
switch, flooding the room with light.

Dianne stood defiantly in front of the wall of cages
housing the exotic birds that had been the only nonfamily
outlet for her love, as well as the only interest she had been
physically able to maintain for too many years of her short

life. She held her bedside lamp like a bludgeon in one hand and pointed toward the bed.

"A rat," she sobbed. "A big rat. He was after my birds."

Barbara saw Zack relax slightly as he took it all in, but it was Mickie who spoke. "No way, Dianne. No rat is going to get caught sixteen floors up, even if he was smart enough to figure out how to get here."

"That's easy for you to say. You didn't wake up and find him getting ready to eat Appolonia and Didacticus. Just look under the bed, Mickie, and see. Oh, shoot him, Zack. Shoot him."

"Mickie—"

Zack's attempt at a warning came too late. Mickie had already dropped to her knees, peering under the bed.

"Nope, no rat," Barbara heard over the sounds of men pouring into the hallway behind her. "But this is the biggest cat I've ever seen."

"Tesla," she heard Zack whisper as Taylor Adams skidded to a halt beside Meg.

A smile softened the too-often-suspicious features of Zack's security chief. "A false alarm?" he asked.

Zack nodded. "Obviously. The only question now is, how did he get up here?"

"Tesla," Barbara murmured as she watched Mickie coax the cat from under the bed. "He's so big," she said, knowing she might not have recognized him, seeing nothing of the tiny little creature she had once taken in except the strange guard hairs that still stood out from his gray-striped coat. "You kept him."

Zack turned toward her, reaching for her, almost touching her. "I— He belonged to you, didn't he?" he said, drawing back. "Of course I kept him."

"Do you know this cat, Mom?" Mickie asked, scampering up from the floor with the unexpected visitor in her arms. "Good grief, he weighs a ton."

"I used to know him, a long time ago," Barbara told her, reaching for her old friend. But he hissed at her, reaching out, batting a claw at her, drawing a single drop of blood. Barbara stepped back, denying the hurt of his betrayal. Af-

ter all, years had passed. Why should the grown cat re
member the woman the kitten had loved?

"Too much excitement," Zack said, obviously trying to
gloss over the rejection. He took the cat from Mickie and
handed him to Taylor. "Take him back downstairs and lock
whatever door he managed to get open this time, will you?"

"Sure, boss," Taylor told him, taking the cat in his arms.
He flashed Meg a rueful grin before turning back to his
men, and with a nod, silently directing them to leave.

Meg walked to her daughter and relieved her of the lamp
before hugging her. "I don't think we have to worry too
much about your lungs anymore, do we sweetheart?"

"Ah, Mom, I didn't mean to scream the house down."

"That's all right, Dianne," Zack told her. "You did the
right thing. In fact, I want you to promise me that any time
anything scares you like this, you won't be afraid to do the
same thing again."

Barbara hugged her valiant daughter, who had obviously
been the first to respond to Dianne's scream. Tomorrow
would be soon enough to urge her to be more careful.
"Bedtime," she whispered, and gave her a nudge toward her
own room. But when she turned to say her own hesitant
good-night to Zack, she found him already gone.

Tesla. Zack had kept that stray scrawny cat that he had
once barely tolerated. *He belonged to you, didn't he? Of
course I kept him.* Barbara hugged her arms as his words
washed over her. Comforted by them, for a moment she al
lowed herself to wonder what else he had kept, until she re
membered that she couldn't let it matter.

Four

Taylor Adams sat at Dianne's place at the breakfast table the following morning. "She's resting," Meg said when Mickie asked about her. "I thought after all her activity last night, she might need a couple of extra hours of sleep."

"Does she need to see a doctor?" Zack asked.

Meg shook her head. "I don't think so. She's so much stronger than she was just a year ago."

Barbara recognized the determined lift of Meg's chin and the barely noticeable moisture in her eyes.

"She's almost—" Meg drew herself back from what Barbara knew to be painful memories of the first years of Dianne's life. "She'll be fine," Meg said. "Just fine. But thank you for asking. And thank you for being so understanding last night."

Barbara saw Taylor Adams relax long enough to smile reassuringly at Meg. But the smile was brief, and the cessation of tension at the table equally brief.

The only one who didn't seem to be affected was Mickie,

as she ate her way through a stack of Mrs. Thompson
pancakes covered with homemade blackberry syrup.

Something was definitely wrong, Barbara thought. Zac
looked even more harried than he had the night before. B
he wasn't going to tell her why. She knew that as certain
as she knew that his security chief was as aware of th
problem as Zack was, which meant it concerned more tha
some glitch in engineering or research and development.

Meg dropped her napkin beside her half-finished breal
fast with a sigh. "I've got to get to work, but I need yo
help, Mickie."

Mickie looked up from the lake of syrup she had con
structed and the pancake dam she was about to destroy, ar
grinned. "Again?"

Barbara watched the interchange between her daught
and her friend, relieved that Meg, in spite of her wor
about Dianne, seemed almost normal again. Meg swo
she'd never met a friendly computer, or one that she ev
began to understand; Mickie had never met one that didn
do everything but roll over and purr for her. But it didn't c
any good to encourage her daughter too much. Barbara ha
little trouble fighting her reluctant smile, although sl
thought maybe laughter might help ease the tension at th
table. "How much did you lose this time?" she asked.

"Just the last twenty pages," Meg said. "And I swear
don't know what I did. I told it to print hard copy and sav
my file and all it did was beep at me."

Mickie demolished the dam and stuffed the oversize bi
into her mouth. "No problem," she mumbled around th
pancakes and a huge swallow of orange juice.

"May I be excused?" she remembered to ask just as sl
reached the breakfast-room door several steps ahead
Meg.

Barbara nodded.

"And, Mom, will you tell Mr. Jameson where I am?"

Again Barbara nodded. And found herself left alone wi
two silent men. She leaned back in her chair, suppressing
sigh, and studied the two of them before turning her atten
tion to Zack. "All right, if you're not going to make co

ersation, I will. Are you going to tell me what's wrong, or
hall I let my fertile imagination work on why the two of you
ook as though you've been involved in a very large argu-
nent?''

Taylor Adams's right eyebrow lifted, but Zack shot him
a look guaranteed to silence him. "Nothing's wrong, Bar-
ara," Zack said evenly. "We're both a little ragged from
vaiting for the next move. That's all.''

"Right.'' Barbara didn't believe that for a minute. She
icked up her coffee cup, debating whether to pursue the
opic or not. Her cup was empty. She set it back in its sau-
er and stood. "If you'll excuse me, I'll leave you two alone
hen, so you can discuss what's not wrong.''

No one offered to stop her. At the door she paused and
urned, the words already on her tongue to remind Zack she
ad a valid interest in what was happening. But the words
ied unspoken as she realized that he, of all other persons,
new too well her concern.

Too agitated to remain alone, Barbara fought what she
ad long ago learned to describe as an anxiety attack by
eeking out Mickie and Meg, watching unnoticed from the
oorway as her imp of a daughter once again, patiently,
escribed to Meg the series of computer commands she
eeded to use. She left when Jamie Jameson joined her at
he doorway, summoning Mickie to her lessons, and Meg
uried herself in a massive fictional shootout.

A year's worth of industry journals waited on the deli-
ate desk in her bedroom. Barbara frowned slightly at the
uperficial nature of the information the tutor had sent her,
ut took the stack of magazines to the comfortable chaise
ear the open doors to the garden and settled herself in for
vhat she suspected would be a much-too-quick study. Soon
er slight frown became a real one, and she delved deeper
nto the journals. She'd been afraid to try to maintain any
rofessional contacts for fear they would lead Zack to her,
ut, Lord, she thought as she finally closed the last one, so
nuch had happened in the years she had been gone; she'd
ever be able to catch up with the innovations.

Catch up? Those had been Zack's words, not hers. She had offered to be of help in some way, but that offer hadn't included a monumental retraining. Not when there would be no need for it. Not when she knew she had to leave as soon as she felt she safely could.

So what *could* she do to fill her time? To keep her from wandering into the forbidden territory her heart and thoughts kept taking her? She glanced around the room, noticing the brightness that now filled it, the stillness of the sheer curtains at the doors, and looked down at her watch. Hours had passed since she'd sat down with the journals. Hours in which she had not thought of Zack once, of Mickie, or Wilson Truett. *Hours.*

Maybe she should catch up. Even if she never used the knowledge, acquiring it would be one way to anesthetize herself to a situation that was proving more painful each day.

She drew a deep breath and looked at the small stack of magazines. But she'd have to be organized about it. She'd begin by asking Jamie to bring her the oldest of the journals she'd missed first, by taking note of any new development as it appeared, by asking at that time for additional material on that development. It would be more difficult for her to have to wait for information rather than seeking it out and following each trail in her own peculiar and sometimes convoluted manner, but it would do. It would have to do.

"Mom?"

Barbara bent over Mickie, tucking the sheet carefully around her in their familiar nighttime ritual. "Yes, sweetheart?"

"Why doesn't Zack spend any time with us anymore?"

Barbara's hand stilled on the sheet for a moment and then moved to smooth a curl away from Mickie's cheek. "He does," she said quietly. "We see him at breakfast every day and almost every evening at dinner."

"No, I mean, *time.* Good time. Fun time, like when we first came and he talked to me and taught me to dive. Time like that. Did I do something wrong?"

Barbara's hand stilled again, this time as she fought a wave of frustration and anger at a life they had been forced into by one man's hatred. "No. Of course not. He's just—"

"I know he's *busy*, Mom. But he was busy then, too."

"Yes, he was." How much should she tell Mickie? How much could this precious, precocious child understand? Probably more than she had given her credit for up until now. Mickie's questions had proven that. And how much did she need to know for her own safety? Some, perhaps. Enough so that Zack's own, understandable, self-protective actions didn't cause her any more suspicion.

"Zack is—Zack is worried. A long time ago, he was hurt by a bad man."

"You mean, like the guy beat him up or something?"

Who promised to destroy everything Zack loved. "Or something," Barbara said. "And now that bad man may be trying to hurt him again."

"And that's why Taylor—Mr. Adams—and Jamie and those other men have guns under their jackets and sometimes that Dirty Harry kind of look in their eyes? Like last night, when we were all chasing that huge old cat?"

Jamie, too? That answered her unasked question of where he worked when he wasn't being a tutor, but raised so many more. "You noticed that?" Barbara asked, determined to answer her daughter's question and not her own. And then she realized what else Mickie had revealed. "Just when did you see a Dirty Harry movie?"

"Mom! I'm not a baby anymore."

Barbara leaned closer, gathering Mickie in her arms. "No, you're not, are you? But sometimes I wish you were."

"Is Mr. Adams mean? Or is he a good guy who sometimes has to do mean things?"

Barbara felt a totally inappropriate chuckle fight its way to freedom. "Where on earth do you get all these questions?"

Mickie squirmed until Barbara released her. "I think he likes Meg."

"Who?"

"Mr. Adams. So I need to know if he's one of the good guys."

Taylor Adams and Meg? Barbara dismissed her too quick denial. One of the disadvantages of living with this whiz kid was that Mickie was as perceptive as she was bright. If she had seen something to indicate an attraction between those two, there had been something to see.

"I think he's a good guy, darling. Zack trusts him."

"Okay," Mickie said around a yawn as she scrunched down among the pillows. "Mom?"

What now? Barbara wondered. She had it on good authority that some children only asked for innumerable glasses of water before surrendering to bedtime. Her daughter's thirst seemed just as insatiable, but for information, not liquid.

"Was he really your cat?"

Barbara smiled. This one was going to be fairly easy, if somewhat predictable. "Yes. A long time ago. So long that I'm afraid he doesn't remember me."

"Why did you name him Tesla?" Mickie asked, now visibly fighting sleep.

"Did you ever hear of Nikola Tesla?" Barbara asked.

"Sure." A yawn punctuated the word. "He was that physi-physi— That guy who did really weird things with electricity."

"That's right." This child never ceased to amaze her. "And when Tesla was a little kitten, his coat wasn't as full as it is now, but he already had those wild guard hairs, you know, the ones that stick out from his fur?"

Mickie nodded, her eyes closed, her breathing slowing.

"And he looked just like he had stuck his tail in a light socket," Barbara said softly.

"Still does," Mickie murmured, turning her head on the pillow. "Night, Mom," she said, her voice fading. "Love you. Tell Zack I love him, too."

Barbara lifted her hand from Mickie's pillow and eased herself away from her sleeping daughter, when what she really wanted to do was grab her close and cry for both of them. "No, darling," she whispered. "I won't do that. I *can't* do that. Not even for you."

Unlike the night before, Barbara heard Zack's footsteps as he approached her. She didn't turn but remained at the wall, looking over the distant lights of downtown Houston. A soft breeze whispered past her, still cool, but she knew that too soon even the evening air would be hot and muggy, too uncomfortable for her to enjoy even this simple pleasure.

"Barbara?"

Had she known he would come to her again tonight? Had she *hoped* he would come? Reluctantly she turned and choked back the moan that rose unbidden to her throat. Zack seemed to have aged visibly in the short time since she had last seen him. The lines were drawn more firmly around his mouth. In the dim, reflected light of the garden, his cheeks seemed, if possible, to have begun to hollow. And his eyes—his once glorious dark eyes—now held all the care and pain of the world.

This was what her coming back into his life had done to him.

This was why she had to find some way to leave, soon.

"You look exhausted." She spoke in a low voice although they were alone, although probably no one except the ever-vigilant security staff remained awake in the entire building, and they were all safely tucked away at their stations or in their living quarters on the floor below.

Zack nodded. "But I couldn't sleep. Why are you still awake?"

She felt her lips crook in a smile, but what she felt was far from humor. "Insomnia must be contagious."

Once she would have taken the few steps that separated them, slid her arms around him and comforted him—and have been comforted by him—until the solace they took from each other blocked out the world and all its hateful memories and became more, much more. Now she was not able to do that. Never again would she be able to do that.

She crossed her arms, reflexively hugging herself, and leaned against the wall.

"Have you heard anything?" she asked.

"We—" Zack stepped to the wall, looking out over the city, not at her. "We hope to—expect to—any day now."

"Zack—" Maybe there was hope for them, after all, a strange, perverse kind of hope. "Is it possible—? Could this whole thing have been a coincidence? Surely if . . . if Truett had anything to do with it, he would have made some demand by now. Perhaps it would be safe for Mickie and me to leave."

"And go where?" he asked harshly. "Back to Meg's house and wait?"

"No. Not there," Barbara admitted, realizing that never again would she feel truly safe if she stayed with Meg Riley, if she didn't sever that connection with her past, too. "I don't know where we'd go. Somewhere—far away. Somewhere . . ."

"Somewhere alone?" he asked. "Just the two of you? At the whim and mercy of a madman?"

"No," Barbara whispered. "Alone. But so far away from him that he wouldn't find us."

"And me, Barbara. Would I not be able to find you, either?"

"After all that has happened," she asked, "why would you even want to?"

"Why?" The word sounded choked in the gentle darkness.

She sensed him turning toward her, saw his hand reach out for her. He was going to touch her. Touch her, and she wasn't strong enough to resist what that touch would make her want. She closed her eyes, steeling her senses and her emotions, retreating into herself as she had once, a lifetime ago, learned to do.

"Damn!"

She felt the word in the soft expulsion of his breath against her cheek, opened her eyes and saw his hand, now fisted, poised at her shoulder, until Zack slowly, carefully, lowered it to his side.

He took a step back from her. "I'm sorry," he said formally. He whirled around and clutched the rim of the wall. "No, damn it, I'm not! You're my wife and I'm not sorry for loving you! I'm not sorry for wanting to touch you. But I am sorry that the thought of my touch is so abhorrent to you, that it brings back memories you want to forget, need to forget, may never be able to forget."

Barbara closed her eyes and rubbed her hands over her arms, trying to ward off a chill not caused by the breeze. He loved her. Was that what he was saying? But he shouldn't. He couldn't.

And he thought his touch repulsed her.

Oh, Zack, she said silently, biting her lower lip to keep the words from escaping. *It's not that. Never that.* She wanted to take him in her arms, despite the cost to her, to erase at least that pain for him.

But might it not be easier for him, eventually, if she allowed him to continue to think that?

"Your touch and my daughter," she said, keeping her voice soft, for his ears alone, knowing she could never tell him the real reason she must leave—he'd never accept it— but also knowing she must continue to give him some reason he could accept. She saw the increased tension in the set of his shoulders, in his grip on the ledge. "Isn't it true, Zack? Every time you look at Mickie, aren't you reminded of what you want most to forget?" He remained silent, yet she didn't need his words to know she spoke the truth.

"Let us go, Zack. If you haven't heard anything in the next few days, let us go. For all our sakes."

"I can't," he said.

"Can't? Or won't? And why?"

He turned toward her then, leaning against the wall, looking battle weary but not yet ready to concede defeat. "In some ways the last seven years have seemed to go on forever, an endless, hopeless time of lost trails and erroneous leads and loneliness without you. In another way, it's as though my life ended when you left and only began again the day I brought you back into my home—or what could have been a home before my stepbrother's poison touched it. I know we can never go back to what we were, the way we were, before he intruded. But I can't bear the thought of letting him take you from me, too, and if you leave, he will have done just that."

"Too?" she prompted gently.

"I never told you about him, and I should have. But by the time we met, I thought he had exhausted all his hatred. I thought he had already destroyed all that he could destroy.

"Let me tell you now, Barbara. And then maybe you can forgive me for dragging you into his web.

"I was fifteen when my father married Wilson's mother. She was a beautiful woman, but she died only a few years later. I realize now she was worn down with trying to cope with him, that she had no reserves left to fight the illness that claimed her, in spite of the love my father gave her. Wilson was three years older than I was when he came to live with us, and I— Maybe I wasn't a typical only child, but I was looking forward to having a big brother.

"I'd been pretty isolated, you see. Off to school during the school year and then left pretty much on my own on the estate during holidays with only an old dog and a horse for company most of the time.

"But Wilson didn't want a brother. He didn't want any competition. He didn't want anyone to have anything he didn't have. My dog died first, the victim of a hit and run. My horse was shot. I was told at the time it was by a stray bullet from a careless hunter. By then I suspected Wilson, but I couldn't believe anyone could be that irrationally cruel, and I told myself I was—that I was becoming paranoid. Then later, much later, my father died, in a senseless accident."

"Zack—"

"I couldn't prove anything—no one could—although at that time I did try. Then, five years before I met you, he tried to take control of the company. I won the fight, but he stole the plans for an experimental airplane, almost destroying the company, and disappeared.

"By the time I met you, I thought that Wilson would never return, that it would be safe for me to live again, to love again. I was wrong. And yes," he said, at last admitting the truth of her accusation, "each time I look at Mickie I am reminded of how wrong I was, of what you suffered, of what he has taken and continues to take from me.

"I want to have her tested."

"What?" Barbara asked, confused by his abrupt shift in subject, but only for a moment.

"I want to prove once and for all that she is my child, or that she isn't."

"No."

"No? Why in God's name not?"

She wanted to touch him, as she once would have, to calm him, to emphasize that she was not unaware of or unconcerned about his feelings. Instead she hugged herself more tightly. "Because it would do no good, and could do a great deal of harm."

"To whom?"

"*To whom?* To my daughter," she said. "To Mickie, who is totally innocent of causing any of this hell. If we prove she is your daughter, we only give—him—another target for his hatred. If we prove... If we prove she is... is not your daughter, we brand her forever as the child of a monster. And I won't allow anyone to do that to her. Not anyone. Not even you."

He remained silent, eyes tightly closed, seeing things she knew he didn't want to see. "All right," he said finally. "No testing. So where does that leave us now?"

"I can't stay with you, Zack."

She felt the blows her words inflicted on him.

"Can't? Or won't?" he asked, throwing her earlier question back at her.

"It's the same thing," she said. "I'm not unreasonable, and I'm certainly not crazy enough to expose Mickie or myself unnecessarily. But if we haven't heard something from him in another week, I'm going to ask you to let us leave."

"Barbara—"

She looked up at him sharply, caught by the hesitation in his voice, by the tortured indecision she saw reflected in his features. This was something else Truett had to answer for—something that had been set in motion long before and for which she had been no more important than a pawn in a chess set.

"A week, Zack," she said as firmly as she could, and then turned and walked steadily, rapidly, away from him before her composure and her resolve melted, before he saw the tears she was no longer able to dam flooding her eyes.

Five

Zack leaned against his desk as he watched the videotape of his wife and her daughter at play. Earlier in the tape he had seen Barbara and Mickie at a grocery store, laughing as they selected a treat for Mickie from the bakery. Now they were in a park, again laughing together, Barbara pushing Mickie in a swing. Laughing. Barbara. And for a few brief minutes Zack had seen her as she had been when she'd first captured his attention and snared his body and then his heart.

She was too thin, much too thin, but her body was lithe and healthy. And her fine features were animated with life, with love, and yes, with laughter, instead of frozen in the mask of no emotion that was all she willingly let him see— or that was all she was able to sustain except in rare moments—like the ones this hidden camera had managed to capture and flaunt before him.

The tape ended, and Zack hit the button to rewind it before placing the remote control on the desk beside him. Sometime during the last week he had realized how unnecessary it was to make Taylor leave the room—these tapes, so far, had contained nothing that couldn't be shared with his chief of security—so now they watched together and Zack only had to view each one a single time.

The tapes were progressing backward in time as Wilson—who else could it be?—showed Zack fragments of what he had missed in Barbara's life, as he showed him what could have been—should have been—a major part of Zack's life.

The week Barbara had demanded had passed the day before. Zack had taken the coward's path; he had avoided her. As he had avoided telling her about these tapes. As he wanted to continue to avoid telling her. Because knowing about them could only renew all her fears, all her memories, of a time when she had *known* Wilson was taping her.

Taylor waited in silence until the tape clicked off. Then he stood and walked over to the wall of windows overlooking the downtown skyline. "When do you suppose that one was filmed?" he asked. "A year ago? Longer?"

"Judging from Mickie's size, probably last spring," Zack said, waiting for the questions he knew were sure to come but unwilling to succumb to speculation.

"It's odd, don't you think? No one has had a clue to Truett's whereabouts for years, but someone just happens to be taking candid shots of the one sure way he can get to you."

"And they were candid shots," Zack told Taylor. "Completely unrehearsed. Barbara wasn't acting. She can't lie well enough to act."

"You've forgotten that she lied to Meg Riley and the world for almost seven years," Taylor reminded him.

Zack refused to answer; he had no answer.

"You're going to have to talk to her about this, Zack. To question her about this, and about what she is searching for in the research files. Jamie tells me she has a new list for him almost every day."

"I told you from the beginning that she would be reading up on industry changes."

"And doesn't it also seem odd to you that the industry changes that most interest her are the ones that have also been of the most interest to Gordon Aviation?"

"No." Zack fought back a wave of memories. Now was not the time to explain them other than to extract one pertinent fact. "No, it doesn't seem odd at all, since the seeds for both those interests were planted long ago." In planning sessions, in discussions with Ray Sanders, and more intimately in the privacy of their home, of their bedroom, of their bed.

"Damn it, Zack!" Taylor turned from the window to face him. "I didn't want to tell you. I wasn't going to tell you until I had more facts."

"Tell me what, Taylor?" Zack asked.

"Someone has been in the computer."

"What?"

"It didn't show up until we were going through a routine check of the daily logs. We're checking on authorization now, but it looks as though there have been three or more entries that can't be verified by any of the authorized personnel. And frankly, because of the terminal, I don't think we're going to verify them."

"Which terminal?"

Taylor turned toward Zack's own unit and nodded.

"Mine?" Zack asked, watching his own skeptical reaction to Taylor's statement in the wall-size mirror behind his computer console. And then, rallying, he smiled grimly. "I don't believe anyone's asked me when I was or wasn't using my terminal."

"That's because the times that you've been in your office in the middle of the night, there's been no activity."

"During the night?"

Taylor nodded.

"With your staff on duty?"

"Yeah."

"And no one saw anything suspicious except on a computer printout?"

Taylor glanced at the computer terminal as though asking for answers. Apparently none came to him. He looked back at Zack and spoke evenly. "I'm not proud of the job we've done so far, but I guarantee you, not so much as a speck of dust will move in this building that we won't be aware of in the future. And that still leaves us with the problem of who could breach the system's locks and passwords—not once, but at least three times—and what that person was after."

"And who better than the person who designed the system we used for years before finally upgrading to this one?" Zack asked quietly.

"I wouldn't have said anything until I had more evidence."

"But you would have suspected her."

Taylor nodded. "Who else?"

"That's right, Taylor. Who else? I've warned you about this before. Barbara is innocent. She was and is the victim here. Remember that, or, as much as I have respected you and your work in the past, I'll find someone who will. And in the meantime I expect you to watch her as closely, for her protection, as you apparently have been watching me."

The week had passed. And then a day, and then another. Barbara dragged herself out of bed, forcing herself to face still another. She knew what Zack was doing; he was avoiding her, avoiding the confrontation that neither of them wanted but which seemed inevitable.

Nothing had happened. If it had, he would have told her. And if it hadn't, she had no reason to stay. No reason. In spite of what she might once have wanted. In spite of what her restless dreams and sleepless nights told her she still wanted. In spite of Zack's protestations about her safety, about Mickie's safety.

She dressed hurriedly and went down the hallway to Mickie's room, wondering if she would have to drag her once-up-before-the-crack-of-dawn daughter out of an unrefreshing sleep yet again. It had to be the tension crackling almost visibly through the air that drained Mickie so, a tension that it seemed Barbara could do nothing to alleviate.

Mickie's room, instead of facing the roof garden, had windows overlooking a view of suburban Houston beyond the roof's protective wall. A minuscule stretch of terrace led, she knew from one brief exploration, around the corner in one direction to the garden and in the other to the enclosed mechanical apparatus of the building.

Through the open windows she heard the hum of powerful air-conditioning units and shook her head. The noise wasn't too obvious this far from the units, but she knew even if it had been, Mickie would have the windows open until the south Texas heat, and only that, forced her to close them.

Which would be soon. The month of May was drawing to a close; June, and the true advent of summer, rapidly approached.

She glanced at the bed across the room. Nope. Mickie wasn't up yet. She almost hated to wake her, to drag the child into another day where she had to wonder about the peculiar behavior of the adults surrounding her. But she had to. If she allowed Mickie's routine to suffer because of her own problems, she'd only be doing her daughter an even greater disservice.

Mickie lay curled on her side, facing the wall, the sheet tangled around her feet, her arm crossing her and stretching toward the wall. Barbara sat on the side of the bed and reached for her daughter's shoulder, then drew back, taking a long, incredulous look at what Mickie's outstretched arm covered.

Curled into the curve of Mickie's body, protected by one slender, fragile arm, and snoring loudly enough to rival most full-grown men, lay one very contented and very overweight gray cat.

"Well, hello there," Barbara said softly. "Where did you come from? And better yet, how did you get here?"

"Hmpff?" she heard as Mickie twitched once and settled back into her sleep.

This was one of those moments, those precious moments that seemed to come ever more slowly as Mickie grew older, that she had so often wanted to share—with Zack. Her daughter and the cat that had once been hers, curled together in innocence, finding comfort and companionship with each other, even in sleep. But this was nothing she could share. Especially not with Zack. *Damn!* she thought as she felt her throat thicken and begin to close. She wouldn't feel cheated. And she wouldn't feel the pain of Zack's being cheated. Not when she had Mickie to love and to love her and to depend on her. She wouldn't.

"Mickie?" she said, schooling her voice to its normal level. "Wake up, hon. It's morning."

"Hmpff?" she heard again, but at last Mickie managed to open one eye and turn her head toward her. "Morning?"

"I'm afraid so," Barbara told her. "Time to get up and face the music."

"What music?" Mickie mumbled, still not completely awake until Tesla turned under her arm and stretched. "Uh-oh."

"Uh-oh is right, but if you hurry and get dressed you can catch Mr. Jameson on his way to your class and have him take Tesla wherever it is he belongs before Dianne even realizes this ferocious monster is on the loose again."

"Mo-om," Mickie said, cradling a protective arm around the cat, who repaid her by purring contentedly and kneading his paws against her side. "Tesla wouldn't hurt her birds."

"I know that, and you know that," Barbara said gently. "But Dianne doesn't know it. You know how much those birds mean to her."

"Yeah, I know. But—"

But what? Barbara wondered. Was her daughter about to tell her it was time for her to have something of her own, too? It was. Past time. But there didn't seem to be anything Barbara could do about it yet.

"Yes, I know," Mickie said finally. "And I'm really glad she's got them. I just wish..."

Barbara leaned forward and brushed a kiss across her daughter's sleep-warmed cheek. "I know, sweetheart," she said. "I know."

* * *

But Mickie couldn't have anything of her own, and neither could Barbara, not even the life she had once promised herself, as long as they were trapped like flies in Wilson Truett's web. Or were they? Wouldn't Zack have told her if there had been any move made toward them? Maybe it was Zack's web that held them snared.

The problem was, Zack had apparently again, as he had when he'd first brought her here, abandoned her to the luxury of his penthouse and disappeared. She suspected he was in his office downstairs, but the elevator in the foyer and the door to the service stairs, which she found hidden in a hallway behind the kitchen, had coded keypads in place of conventional locks and, while the service stairs didn't appear to be guarded, the elevator shared the foyer with a graceful English desk and a burly linebacker type who passed the time searching through reams of computer printouts.

Finally she left word with Mrs. Thompson, the housekeeper, Jamie, and even the linebacker in the foyer that she needed to speak with Zack. But dinner passed with no word from him, then early evening, then the hours after she had put Mickie to bed.

Why wouldn't he talk to her? she wondered as she lay back on the chaise in her room, the French doors open to admit the gentle breeze and the soft, nighttime lighting of the patio. Why *should* he? she finally admitted to herself. She had made it clear to him she only stayed because of the threat of physical danger to herself and her daughter. She refused even to discuss staying with him once the threat was passed. And worst of all, but the most necessary for herself and for him if only she could explain why, she had left him with the impression his touch repulsed her.

He had heard nothing from Truett; she was almost certain of that. If he had, he would have warned her.

And if he hadn't . . . For the first time Barbara let herself wonder what her life would be like if once and for all time, finally and forever, Wilson Truett no longer threatened her future. If he were well and truly gone, was there any longer a reason why she *couldn't* stay with Zack? Why she couldn't lose herself in the strength and comfort and passion of his arms as she had longed to do for so long it seemed that each breath she took taunted her with her need? Why she couldn't give voice and freedom and life to the love for him—with him—that had once so completely filled her?

Mickie, a still, small voice reminded her, taunting her for wanting, chiding her for forgetting. Even with all danger gone, Zack would never be able to look at Mickie without remembering, and in an atmosphere without love and security and encouragement, her bright, beautiful daughter would wither, would draw all her enthusiasm and emotion and love and curiosity into a shell of her own making, and would die to the joy that life should hold.

Just like she had.

Barbara felt her own whimper of denial before forcing herself to silence and hiding her face in her hands.

Just like Zack had?

Oh, God, were they all trapped forever in what had once seemed such a necessary lie?

No. If Truett was no longer a threat, she could free Mickie and, to some degree, she could free Zack, too.

She heard a subdued noise from the patio and almost immediately identified it. Water. The soft sounds of a swimmer moving steadily and determinedly through water. With no hesitation, she knew who the swimmer had to be—and what she now had to do.

By the time Barbara convinced her legs to move, Zack had left the pool. His room was at the end of the patio, also facing the pool, with French doors still open to the night. Barbara knew it was his room, although she had never been in it. Now she cautiously stepped through the doors. She heard the sound of the shower in the adjacent bathroom and drew a deep breath. Reprieve. If she wanted it. If she could convince her conscience that she really didn't need to speak.

She couldn't.

Curious, she looked around Zack's private space. Only two things were familiar: a huge eighteenth-century wardrobe they had found at a private auction their first summer

ogether, and an art-nouveau lamp she had fallen in love
vith. Everything else, from the bed to the rug on the floor,
vas new to her but not unfamiliar. The room was the es-
ence of Zack. Tasteful. Understated. Strong. Beautiful.
Honest.

She crossed to the little lamp by what had to be his read-
ng chair and touched its shade, remembering when she had
ound it, how he had teased her about it and then surprised
ier by having it delivered and in place in their room before
hey'd returned from dinner that evening.

He'd done so many things like that for her, and she'd be-
ieved all along—still did—that he had taken genuine delight
n her pleasure... in her... in her love.

She didn't hear him—he made no sound—but she knew
when he entered the room. She dropped her hands to her
sides and turned to face him.

He was wearing a short terry-cloth robe with the towel he
iad used to rough-dry his hair draped over his shoulders.
That habit hadn't changed, although she could see in the
bathroom's light other changes that time had brought
about—the vagrant strands of silver in his still-damp hair
now reflecting the artificial light; the deepening lines running from his eyes—lines once caused by laughter and now
caused by— By what? The—

"Barbara?"

Just that. One word. And in it she heard all the questions he wouldn't ask her.

Drawing in her breath, standing as tall as her scant five
feet of height would let her, she faced him. "You've been
avoiding me," she said softly.

"Yes."

"Why?" she asked.

"I didn't know what to tell you."

Not "I didn't want to tell you," as she had suspected.
How strange. Until now, Zack had always known what to
tell her, and how. Until now, he had been the one person in
her life who understood her well enough to know what and
how to say anything to her. The only person...

Barbara's mother certainly hadn't known what to say to the overly serious little girl Barbara had been. Nor had any of the numerous "uncles" she had known before her ninth birthday when her single mother had apparently decided coping with her was more than she or any man she might meet should be expected to do and had simply not picked her up from a weekend baby-sitter and had vanished. And in vanishing, she had proved herself more adept in at least one thing than her frighteningly bright child: Barbara's mother had never been found.

But Zack...Zack had known from the beginning to treat her as a woman instead of as an intellect packaged in faintly feminine camouflage—a woman with needs and a great ability to pour out the love she had kept locked within her for most of her life.

She didn't remember doing it, but she found that she had raised her hand to her mouth, holding back words she longed to but would never be able to say to him. He was studying her carefully, warily, and she understood why.

She had hurt him—necessarily, but also, she now suspected, unnecessarily in her mistaken need to protect herself and her own from a threat that had never materialized.

And she would never willingly have hurt him; she'd had no choice. Or had she? *Did* she? Not about their lack of a future together, but about what their past had meant.

She saw his eyes narrow in a frown and his hand reach tentatively toward her as she felt the moisture of tears threatening to fall. She stifled her moan and twisted away from him in a futile attempt to hide her weakness from him, only to see him jerk his hand back and tense as though she had struck him.

No! she cried silently. *No more lies. At least, not about this.*

But she knew Zack well enough to understand that mere words from her would not dispel the one lie she had allowed to build between them, and that she could no longer allow to torment this man who had taught her how to love, and how to accept love.

She dropped her hand from her mouth and tilted her head upward to look at him. Pain, anguish, regret—she saw all of those in his eyes—and a smoldering need that almost frightened her by its intensity. Choking back that fear, concentrating on only the love Zack had once so selflessly given her, she took a step toward him, then another, and another, until she stood only a breath away from him.

Then, as she had needed to do all those long, lonely years, she swayed forward, feeling his small start of surprise and renewed tension as at last, once again, she allowed herself the luxury of leaning against his strength.

She heard the race of his heart beneath her cheek, felt his arms raise and then drop once again to his sides, heard the confusion in his voice. "Barbara, what are you doing?"

She slid her arms around his waist, felt the muscles of his back, still tense and unyielding beneath her hands. "Please, Zack, just hold me." *And let me hold you.* But she could never tell him that, never let him know her need to hold him, to answer his unvoiced plea, was almost as great as her need to be held.

"But my touch..."

Is heaven. Is agony. "I lied. Please, Zack."

And at last she felt his arms tentatively embrace her, and heard his words, choked and hesitant. "You don't have to beg—never that. Don't you know, my sweet Barbara, how much I have wanted to hold you, how empty my life has been without you in it, how afraid I was that I'd have to spend the rest of my life just as empty, just as alone, without you?"

"Don't, Zack." And yes, she did have to beg, at least for his understanding. "This is not about yesterday or tomorrow—it can't be—it's only about now."

She felt his arms tighten possessively around her, his hands at her nape and the small of her back press her closer against the still tense strength of his chest and against the arousal he made no effort to hide from her.

She felt his deep sigh, almost a moan, as he released her, as he lifted his hands to cup her face and hold it still as he looked down at her, as he bent toward her. His lips took hers in a moment that stopped time, sensation, even her heart, before all burst forth in vibrant, pulsating life such as she had not known since one morning frozen forever in her memory when she had left him for what was to have been only a brief, necessary separation in downtown Atlanta.

She felt her own moan and clutched at his back, trying to get ever closer to him as his mouth continued to claim hers in welcome, in celebration, and finally in surrender to the desire she felt tightening his body.

He tore his mouth from hers, and she felt his lips touch her eyelids, her cheeks, her hair, before his arms went once again around her, drawing her tightly to him, and his mouth once again sought hers. No longer restrained by the fear of repulsing her, his body remembered too well what had pleased hers.

She felt his tongue probing her lips and opened unhesitatingly to the remembered pleasure and the shared need. She felt his hand on her breast, and her heart seemed to stop before racing on again, outstripping the heavy pulsing that seemed to thrum through her, from her breast, to her belly, to her womb. And all the while her thoughts, as unrestrained as her body, were crying *Yes, yes. Oh, please, yes. Let me have at least this much before I have to leave him again,* while her tears ran unchecked and unnoticed across her cheek, into her hair, down her throat. Until Zack felt them.

He looked down at her, tracing gentle thumbs along the paths of her tears. "I've never seen you cry," he said wonderingly, and then, unable to hide the bitter regret in his expression or in his voice, he pressed her cheek to his chest. "I never wanted anything to hurt you. I would have given my life to keep you from harm. I still will. I promise you. He— no one will ever hurt you again."

What was he saying? His words seemed to come from a great distance away, cushioned as she was in the cloud of need that enveloped her, but slowly they did penetrate that cloud and then slammed into her. *Hurt her? Who?*

Had she been mistaken? Had Zack's silence not meant what she thought? Had she admitted her desire and, in so doing, her love for Zack at a time when that was the worst thing—the *one* thing that she must hide from him at any cost? Even the pain that lying to him would cost—*had* cost—both of them?

She forced her wayward hands to release him, to fall to her sides; forced her body to straighten away from his even while still held in his embrace; forced her voice to deny the emotions that raged through her. "You've heard something?"

Not understanding, Zack traced his hands from her cheeks to her arms, caressing them as he attempted to draw her closer. "Don't worry," he murmured. "There's nothing for you to worry about."

"You've heard something!"

Zack looked down at her, his eyes probing hers, seeing too much and yet, she prayed, not enough.

"I thought..." Her voice failed her, and she had to turn her face away from his before she could continue. "I thought that when you failed to say anything at the end of the week it meant you had heard nothing, that you were remaining away until you could find a way to convince me to stay. I thought..."

His silence told her how futile that hope had been. Reluctantly she looked up at him; reluctantly she stepped away. And he let her go, his arms dropping to his sides in weary resignation.

"Tell me," she said. "Tell me!"

He shook his head and raked his hand through his hair. He looked at his hand as though surprised to find his hair still damp from his forgotten shower before grasping her shoulders. "I promised you no one will hurt you again. Can't you trust me to do that?"

She drew in a deep, shuddering breath, closed her eyes briefly, and then found that she was hugging herself, warming her crossed arms with her restless hands. "What have you heard?"

Zack took a step back from her, still holding her, and he, too, drew a deep breath. "No," he said. "Apparently you can't. And I don't suppose you have any reason to."

"Zack..." But Barbara knew even as she whispered his name that she couldn't reassure him. Neither of them could afford for her to do that. "Tell me what's happened."

"We've had a message," he told her, but he looked away from her, unable to meet her eyes. "We don't even know if it's from Wilson. And that is all I can tell you now."

"Or all you *will* tell me?"

Releasing her completely, he stepped back from her, but putting more than just the few feet of space that separated them between them.

"*Now* didn't last very long, did it?" he asked, and she heard defeat in his voice to echo the defeat she felt in her heart.

"No," she said softly, feeling the weight of still more yet-unshed tears in her throat. "We should have known it couldn't."

Six

Barbara...

Her dreams that night, when she finally managed to sleep, were haunted—by Zack, by the sound of his voice, by the memory of his touch. She awoke later than usual and not quite clear-headed. She hurried to Mickie's room to get her ready for the day, only to discover that, for a change, her daughter was already up and gone.

She found Mickie at the breakfast table, where everyone else had already gathered by the time she arrived. Everyone but Zack. Just after she had seated herself, he came into the room looking crisp and powerful and refreshed, with Taylor Adams following him like a battle-weary shadow.

Zack bent to her and placed a light kiss on her lips. "Good morning."

Startled, Barbara jerked back from him. "What are you doing?" she whispered.

Zack grinned at her in satisfaction and with a vaguely predatory gleam in his dark eyes, but he spoke softly so that only she would hear. "What I should have been doing since the day I found you again, and what I intend to continue to do now that I know that you still want me."

"Zack—"

He straightened away from her and seated himself in the chair next to hers. "I left something in your room," he said pleasantly. "I want you to wear them."

"Zack?"

"Good morning, Meg," he said, casually avoiding Barbara's questioning eyes and just as casually avoiding looking at either of the two children. "Have you lost any more pages into the dungeons of your computer lately?"

Meg glanced at the two of them, frowned slightly, and tried to cover it with a chuckle. "Not lately. And not, thank God, irretrievably. I did lose a book once," she said. "A whole manuscript. I don't know what I would have done without Barbara. She found it in some directory I didn't even know I had and then lectured me for the next week about the need to back everything up."

Seated across the table beside Meg, Taylor cleared his throat and Barbara saw his dark brows draw into a frown before he noticed her glance and cleared his expression. Taylor and Meg? Barbara remembered Mickie's comments. Maybe. And, if so, was that frown caused by nothing more than his concern to shield Meg from their teasing? Somehow his glower had seemed much more ominous than that. But if not that, then what?

"And then Mom taught me how to help her," Mickie said, oblivious to any undercurrents. "That's a really neat computer you let Meg use, Zack. It's way more powerful than she needs, though. Now, I—"

"Mickie." Torn between Mickie's enthusiasm and Zack's apparent indifference to her daughter, Barbara cautioned the child to silence.

"But, Mom—"

Barbara shook her head and gave her daughter her not-now look before glancing at Zack just in time to see the pain in his eyes before he masked it.

"Does she need one?" Zack asked, meeting Barbara's eyes.

"Oh, yes, please, Zack—"

"No," Barbara told him, interrupting her daughter, who seemed oblivious to the fact that Zack was doing his best to ignore her presence. "You've been more than generous already. Neither of us needs anything more."

He nodded and abruptly pushed up from his chair. "I've changed my mind," he said, dropping his hand to her shoulder, and she felt a flush of heat run through her. "I'm not hungry for breakfast, after all."

"What was that about?" Taylor asked as they waited in the foyer for the elevator.

Ignoring him, Zack looked at the member of Taylor's staff who had risen when they'd approached but had immediately reseated himself at the desk and resumed his study of the computer printouts. "Have you learned anything new?"

Taylor shook his head. "Not a damn thing. There was one call from outside, but it could have been a wrong number. There didn't seem to be any attempt to actually access the computer."

The elevator doors slid open and Zack strode into the small car. Pushing the one option on the control panel, he remained silent while Taylor entered the car until the doors opened one floor below into the reception area of his private suite of offices.

"No other tapes arrived?"

"No, Zack. You know I would have told you."

"No word on Wilson's whereabouts?"

"No."

"No additional suspects for your list of supposed conspirators?"

Taylor shook his head once, abruptly, and his eyes flashed a quick burst of frustration and anger. "Are you dissatisfied with my work? Is that what all these questions are about? I know we haven't made any headway. Do you want my resignation?"

Zack dragged his thoughts back to his security chief. "No. Of course not."

"Then what do you want?"

Want? Zack remembered the fragile strength of Barbara's shoulder beneath his hand, the smooth, warm touch of her lips beneath his, the surprise in her eyes when he had kissed her openly in front of everyone—and the despair in them as she had watched him try to deal with his feelings about Mickie. *Want?* He wanted more than he would ever be able to order even someone as skillful as Adams to get for him.

"Tell Jamie to get the girls a computer," he said, closing away what he really wanted. "Have him load it up with all the games he can find and anything else he thinks girls that age might want."

"Zack—"

"And tell your team I expect results. Soon."

Her wedding rings.

Barbara found them in a jeweler's box on her desk beside the new stack of material Mrs. Thompson, the housekeeper, had delivered from Jamie.

She held the box open in her hand, feeling her pulse beating heavily in her throat, feeling the pressure of tears behind her eyes, feeling the tightening of her heart in her chest.

She hadn't seen the engraved gold band or the diamond solitaire engagement ring for seven years, had reconciled herself to never seeing them again. Now, with no warning, she held them in her hand.

But, yes, she had been warned.

I left something in your room. I want you to wear them.

This was madness, she thought as she lifted the rings from their nest and set the empty box on the desk. Madness. But, oh, she had been so happy when Zack had first placed these rings on her finger. Happy, and proud. And so naively sure that life would hold only good things for the future as long as she had Zachary Gordon by her side.

"Mom?"

Startled out of her reverie, Barbara almost dropped the rings. Clutching them in her fist, she twisted around to find her daughter at her side, a look of awe in her innocent eyes.

"Wow. They really are gorgeous. I didn't know you still had them."

"*Still?*" Barbara opened her fist and looked at the rings. "What do you mean, *still?*"

Mickie averted her eyes. Now the innocence in them was clearly forced. Barbara dropped onto the desk chair and clasped her daughter's shoulders. "How do you know about the rings, Mickie? Have you been...?" Oh, Lord, she thought she'd long ago broken Mickie of this one bad habit. "Have you been exploring again?"

Mickie grimaced. "Zack's room," she mumbled.

"Zack's room," Barbara repeated flatly. "Mickie, how could you? We are guests in his home. We don't have any right to invade his privacy."

"But, Mom, I just wanted to see where he *really* lives. And there's this stupendous big old chest in there, and all I did was open the door to see if it is as neat on the inside as it is on the out, and there is this really great-looking carved box just inside, and this picture of you and him right on top, almost, when I opened that, and it was your *wedding* picture, and you'd never told me about *that,* and he kissed you this morning in front of me and everyone, and are we going to stay here now or what?"

Barbara felt laughter and sobs both building within her. She pulled Mickie into her arms, hiding her face in her child's clean, sweet-smelling hair, and fighting her tears. She had to chastise her for invading Zack's privacy, but she had to answer her, too. She could no longer avoid at least part of the truth.

"We're going to stay here a little while longer," she said slowly. "But then... then we're going away."

"But you're married. I saw the picture. And when people are married, they live together."

"Mickie. Oh, Mickie." Would this be it? The moment when her heart finally broke in two? "That picture was taken a long time ago. Things happen. People change."

"You mean, like Zack changed since we got here?"

Barbara couldn't hold back one shuddering breath as she hugged her daughter fiercely and then forced herself to loosen her grasp. "More than that, darling. Much more than that."

"Mom?" Mickie asked, squirming for freedom and twisting to look at Barbara's face. "Did that bad man have anything to do with those changes, too?"

Barbara felt the color and warmth draining from her. Oh, God. She'd always had to stay alert to keep ahead of Mickie's fertile mind, but until now she had managed to do just that. Now what did she do? She couldn't lie to her daughter, and she could no longer refuse to answer her. She bit at her lower lip once and willed her voice to be steady.

"Yes, darling," she said finally. "He did."

Mickie's eyes clouded and her sweet mouth twisted in the pout that signaled she was fighting tears. "Then why don't Taylor and Jamie find him and . . . and beat him up . . . and . . . and put him in jail?"

"Because life doesn't always work the way . . . the way we want it to," Barbara said softly.

"But that's not fair. I want to stay with Zack. I want him to like me again. I want us to have a family like the kids at school have. I want . . ."

Oh, my darling, so do I. But Barbara couldn't say that to her daughter. Instead she pulled her into her arms as Mickie collapsed in tears against her, fighting the sobs that threatened to consume her as completely as the ones that now racked the precious little body she held.

She couldn't concentrate. Hours later, Barbara still held the image of her daughter sobbing against her, crying for the family they couldn't have.

Restless, she glanced at her watch and decided it was late enough in the afternoon to risk looking in on Meg. If all had gone well with her writing that morning, she would be finished with her work; if it hadn't, Barbara knew she would welcome the interruption.

But she felt strangely reluctant just to go to Meg needy for companionship, especially in light of the changes Barbara had sensed in Meg since Meg had learned her true identity. It seemed, somehow, inappropriate, even though the two women had developed what Barbara considered a deep friendship rather than an employer-employee relationship over the years. So she went first to the foyer, where their forwarded mail was brought daily.

The man on duty glanced at her questioningly when she walked up to the fragile desk. She offered him a tentative smile. "Has Mrs. Riley picked up her mail today?"

He shook his head and surprised her by grinning. "Not yet. I hope this means she's worked her way out of that bad spot she was in."

A bad spot? Meg had told a virtual stranger she was having trouble with her writing and hadn't mentioned it to her? "I do, too," she said, not giving voice to her surprise over this unexpected comment. "Did either of us get any mail today?" She wouldn't have; she never did. But this was another subterfuge she suddenly felt it necessary to perpetuate.

The man nodded and reached for a stack on the credenza behind him—a box, three padded mailers, and half a dozen or so business-size envelopes. "It looks like maybe her copies of her new book are here," he said as he hefted the box. "She promised me I could read a copy when they came in. You don't think she'll forget?"

"She won't forget," Barbara told him as she held out her arms for him to place the packages in them. "Meg never forgets a promise."

"Are you sure you can handle all this?"

Surprised yet again, this time by the kindness in the big man's voice, Barbara smiled at him. "I'm sure," she said softly.

Meg's door was open—just a crack—a sure sign that she was searching for an excuse to abandon her computer. Barbara shifted the armload of mail and tapped gently. "Meg?"

She heard the muffled noise from inside that was Meg's usual oh-please-bother-me response and eased the door open. "You have mail," Barbara said cheerfully, scooting the whole pile onto a table. She spoke with the knowledge of long familiarity with Meg's mail. "It looks like author's copies, galleys, the contracts you've been expecting, and maybe—" she shifted the padded mailers and lifted the largest one, weighing it in her hands "—maybe line edits to review. Lots of good, legitimate procrastination to get you away from whatever corner you've written yourself into now."

Meg looked up at her and grinned, running one hand through her by now thoroughly disheveled long black hair. "Why did I ever let you in on my secrets?" she asked. "You were so much nicer to me when you were still in awe of the writing process."

"Awe?" Barbara asked. "In awe of a woman who spends her afternoons telling tales, spinning stories, weaving webs without benefit of yarn or fiber?"

"All right. All right," Meg said, laughing. "Give me the letters and an excuse to turn this monster off for the day."

Barbara shook her head, delighted to see again her friend's quick humor and teasing manner. She looked at the monitor, at the cursor blinking at the end of a line near the center of the screen. "Are you really stuck?" she asked, walking closer.

"Meg?" she asked as she recognized the words on the screen. "Isn't this—?"

With quick, jerky gestures, Meg closed the file and blanked her copy from the screen.

"Too late," Barbara told her, feeling a sense of guilt that she knew she could never more than partially allay. "I already recognized it. That's the same material Mickie recovered for you days ago, isn't it?" She captured a footstool and scooted it close, sitting so that she faced Meg. "Why didn't you tell me you were having this much trouble? I knew this situation had to be hard on you, but I didn't dream it had you completely blocked. How can I help?"

Meg looked at her, all traces of laughter gone from her troubled eyes. "It isn't your fault, Barbara. Honest. I—I do this sometimes."

"Sure," Barbara told her. "And I'm so obtuse, I've never noticed before. Meg, I know—I know you're confused, maybe even angry about why I kept my past secret from you—"

"No—"

"I think yes—"

"Barbara, damn it!" Meg spun her chair, jerking away from even visual contact with Barbara. "Believe me, it's—Your not telling me about your past has nothing to do with why I haven't been able to write. Trust me. Please...please trust me." She sighed and once again turned to face Barbara, dredging up a lopsided grin. "And give me the mail."

Barbara recognized Meg's efforts to dismiss their painful topic and decided to honor them, for now. Reverting to her earlier teasing banter, she walked to the table and sorted through the small assortment of envelopes.

"Okay. Which do you want first? Agent? Editor? It's not your birthday, so this must be an invitation. Oh, and look. Here's another letter from that publisher who keeps trying to woo you away from—" She glanced up to see Meg clenching the arms of her chair, her face as pale as the white silk shirt she wore. "Meg? What's wrong?"

"Nothing."

"Nothing? Then why do you look like you're going to pass out?"

"It's nothing, I said." Meg pushed herself up from the chair, catching hold of its arms while she visibly steadied herself. "I'm sorry, Barbara, I—" She glanced around the room, at anything, Barbara suspected, to keep from meeting Barbara's own questioning glance. "I promised Dianne I'd spend this afternoon with her. And I think...I think I'm probably late. You know how she gets when she thinks I've forgotten her."

Barbara dropped her hands to her sides. Meg had chosen the one excuse she couldn't argue with. Dianne was the model of decorum except when her birds or her mother's promises were concerned. She nodded once and stepped back, letting Meg walk past her from the room but promising herself that she would do everything in her power to free Meg from the trap she herself could not escape.

Mickie was not in her room, which was just as well, Barbara thought. She wasn't at all sure she was strong enough for more of her daughter's questions. And after her confrontation with Meg, solitude seemed almost welcome. But her room wasn't empty, she learned as she entered from the hallway. Mrs. Thompson was there, hanging a garment bag in her closet, and a department store package rested on the bed.

Mrs. Thompson turned from the closet, closed the door and scooped up the package, walking briskly to the dresser where she opened a drawer and started placing lacy undergarments inside before she noticed Barbara standing in the doorway. She smiled at her in the mirror and continued with her work. "The rest will be delivered tomorrow, Mrs. Gordon," she said. "But Mr. Gordon was emphatic about having at least this much by this evening."

Mrs. Gordon? The woman usually avoided addressing her by any name. And was that what appeared to be—a genuine smile? How strange. But then, this whole day had been strange.

"What will be delivered, Mrs. Thompson? And what is 'this much'?"

"Oh. I thought you must have known. The rest of your clothes, of course. Mr. Gordon sent me shopping right after breakfast this morning. I've put the dress and shoes for your dinner tonight in the closet, and I'll bring the rest tomorrow after Mr. Jameson's people bring them up."

"Dinner?" Barbara asked quietly, although the housekeeper seemed to find nothing strange in her voice. "Tonight?"

Mrs. Thompson smiled at her again. "Yes, at nine o'clock." She closed the dresser door and turned, still smiling. "Now, I've got to hurry if I'm going to have the young ones fed in time for you to get Mickie tucked in bed before your own supper."

* * *

This is madness, Barbara thought again later that night as she faced herself in the mirror. Sheer madness. But she ran a caressing hand over the sensuous emerald silk dress she wore. Zack had not selected it; she forced herself to remember that one fact—but he could have; the style was his taste, and hers. From a halter top and deliciously bare back, the dress draped in slender, graceful folds to the floor. The same madness that kept her from telling Zack she would not have dinner with him and had guided her hands while she'd clothed herself in lace and silk had also steadied her hands as she'd applied the new makeup she found in her bathroom—the same brands, the same shades as she had once worn, and as she had dried and styled her hair and left it loose and flowing down her back.

She felt slightly wicked and very feminine—both alien feelings to the Barbara she had become.

Madness.

She clutched her left hand in her right, running her fingers over the rings she had been unable to keep from putting on—just for a little while.

The knock on her hallway door jerked her back into the present and all the reasons why she shouldn't be doing what she was very much sure she was going to do. But before she had time to work herself into doubts and indecision and a thoroughly, but protective, argumentative mood, Zack opened the door and stepped into her room, closing the door behind him.

Barbara's breath caught in her throat. She had seen him in evening dress before, many times, but she never ceased to marvel at how well he wore the formal black suit. She recognized the gold studs and cuff links he wore in his white, silk, pin-tucked shirt; she had given them to him. But the gold watch was new. And the ring? Oh, God. She bit back a sob. Now he, too, wore his wedding ring.

She clutched her left hand, wanting to hide her rings, needing to hide her weakness from him. "Zack—"

He shook his head. "Don't, Barbara. Not tonight. We'll argue all you want later, but give us tonight."

Would she be forever damned for agreeing to his request? Probably. But she couldn't deny him. And she couldn't deny herself. She wanted this memory, this . . . illusion, too much. She nodded her head in silent acceptance and watched some of the tension leave his body.

Reaching into an inside jacket pocket, he withdrew a small package and crossed the room, handing it to her. "I was going to give you this in Charleston," he said. "But somehow you managed to distract me."

She remembered too well how she had distracted him and felt a blush rising. "*I* distracted *you?*" she asked as she took the package, a jeweler's box, from him. "One of us must have a faulty memory. Oh, Zack—"

She held the open box in her hand, staring mesmerized at the antique topaz earrings she had once admired. "These are too much—I can't—"

"You can," he said insistently. "You know how much you wanted them. You know how much I wanted to give them to you."

Oh, yes, she had wanted them. She had wanted them because he told her that the topaz stones brought out the dark honey and gold streaks in her blond hair, that they warmed her skin and the golden lights in her hazel eyes until she reminded him of a sleek, tawny, self-confident lioness. She had wanted them because when she had held them up to her ears and looked toward Zack for approval, she had seen *him* wanting *her.*

Her hands shook as she reached to lift one long pendant from the jeweler's box.

"Let me," Zack said, covering her hands with his as he took the box from her. He set it on the dressing table and lifted one earring from it. Gently he brushed her hair away from her ear, and Barbara felt the weight of it shift against her back, bared now by the halter style of the green silk dress he had given her, she felt the caress of his hands as he inserted the tiny post of the earring in her ear and twisted the tiny, protective back into place, felt the tingle that started with his touch on the shell of her ear and spread through her, warming her, weakening her.

He touched the pendant lightly, shifting it, allowing it to fall free, and in so doing, brought his fingers, equally lightly, down and across the sensitive hollow behind her ear, her cheek, her throat. He moved and Barbara forced herself to breathe, but he had only twisted so that he could reach her other ear.

Again she felt the kiss of her hair on her bare back, the loving strokes of his fingers against her ear, her cheek, her throat as Zack ministered to her in a way she had never before dreamed could be erotic.

He stood so close, she smelled the mint of his toothpaste as his breath stroked the delicate skin of her throat, smelled the light spice of his after-shave, felt the warmth emanating from him, heard the beat of his heart growing heavier, growing faster.

"Zack..."

Bringing a trembling hand to rest on her bare shoulder, he took half a step back from her, smiling gently, as though none of the sensations that had racked her—that she had felt coursing through him—had touched him.

"I think dinner is waiting," he said, and if she hadn't once known him so well, she would have heard nothing but calm confidence in his voice.

But she had known him. And he had known her. And if the signs of his desire cried to her from his unspoken words, were hers calling to him, telling him more than she would ever willingly say?

"Dinner," she said, stepping away completely, breaking, for now at least, the physical contact.

He led her to the rooftop garden through the French doors of her room. The garden was deserted; Barbara saw no other person. But while she had dressed behind closed draperies, someone had transformed the penthouse rooftop into a magical place.

The small table in the arbor where she had first confronted Zack had been covered by a linen cloth, a cluster of candles in delicate hurricane-type globes, and two crystal wine flutes. The soft, underwater lighting of the pool and other carefully placed and protected candles among the lush plantings provided subdued lighting against the backdrop of the lights of the Houston skyline in one direction and the darker night sky of the other. Soft music whispered from hidden speakers, and a trolley sat near the table with its silver covers protecting what must be the dinner Zack had planned.

Barbara stopped just outside her door as, without warning, her daughter's words of earlier that day assaulted her.

That's not fair. I want to stay with Zack. I want us to be a family. I want...

Oh, so do I, Barbara thought, fighting a wave of pain. *So do I.*

"Oh, my," she said on a soft, indrawn breath. "It's... beautiful."

Zack took her hand and pressed it into the crook of his arm as he led her to the table. "I hoped you'd think so," he said. He pulled out a chair for her, and Barbara sank onto it, not sure how long her legs would continue to support her.

Barbara recognized the label of her favorite Riesling as Zack lifted a bottle from the silver wine bucket and filled their flutes.

"To... to *now*," he said.

She heard the roughness of his voice and knew he was no more confident than she was, no less affected by the night than she was, no less needy of what the night might bring them than she was.

I want... Oh, God, she wanted. And needed. Could it be so wrong, could it bring so much harm if just once, she took? And gave?

Her hand trembled as she lifted her glass to touch his; her voice faded to almost nothing.

"To now," she promised.

Seven

To now.

The words whispered around them, filling the night air like the soft music, the gentle breeze.

To now.

Was this night, then, all they were ever to have together again?

_No!_

Zack's mind screamed the silent denial of that thought even as it stored up memories—Barbara, slender and sylphlike in the green silk that so lovingly caressed her body; Barbara, wearing his rings and the topaz earrings he had kept safe for her for seven years; Barbara, with her hair loose and flowing across the tender flesh of her bare back, longer than he had ever seen it but with the humidity of the south Texas night already causing it to begin to twist and curl into the ringlets she professed to hate but that he had loved to run his fingers through.

Barbara. Her eyes alive and glowing in the subdued light.

Her laughter soft, and warm, and genuine. Her desire for him at last as real and unhidden as his for her.

Barbara. Less than a foot away from him at the tiny table. Close enough to touch. And for tonight, wanting his touch.

Now he was afraid. Afraid of frightening her. Afraid of hurting her. Afraid of reminding her.

Afraid that this was his only chance to convince her to stay with him. Afraid that nothing he could do or say would bind her to him.

He saw her surprise as he stood, as he took the crystal flute containing still another of her favorites, an after-dinner desert wine, from her fingers, as he took her hands in his and drew her to her feet, facing him but so close she had to tilt her head to watch his eyes, sharing with her breath the air he, too, breathed.

"Dance with me," he said.

Sighing, she leaned forward, resting against him. "Yes."

He fought the tremor in his hands when he took her in his arms and then abandoned the fight. Why shouldn't he let her know he was moved by their closeness? Why shouldn't he let her know that in this, too, he was as vulnerable as she?

The music spun around them, gilding the night air with the poignant melody of a song of lost love as Zack led her into the first tentative steps of the dance, as their bodies brushed and touched and grew painfully sensitive to the closeness of each other, as Zack grew ever more aware that this touching, this closeness, was only a prelude to the intimacy, the sharing, that he needed as much as he needed the air he breathed.

Their steps slowed as their heartbeats accelerated, until, finally, they stood together, locked in a light embrace, unable to continue the dance, unable to separate.

Zack looked down at Barbara's upturned face, at what he prayed was need he saw in the golden lights in her eyes. No longer able to restrain himself, with a groan he bent to her, covering her mouth with his, drinking greedily from the sweetness, the love, that was his by the promises they had once made each other.

He felt her melt against him, answering his need, slipping her arms around his neck, stretching to fit her body more closely to his. Groaning again, when what he really wanted to do was laugh in joy, in triumph, he tightened his arms around her, lifting her closer, deepening the kiss until he felt himself spinning out of control—too soon, much too soon. He tore his mouth from hers and planted welcoming kisses along her jaw, her throat, her forehead, her eyelids. And felt the tears. Sliding quietly, unchecked, from beneath her closed eyes.

"Barbara, I—" he choked out. Oh, God, why now, for the first time in years, had he forgotten the deep emotional scars she must bear? "I'm sorry. I never meant—I would never hurt you—"

"Shh," she whispered, lifting her hands to frame his face, to draw light, loving fingertips across his lips. "I know who you are, my—Zack. I've always known the difference."

The world spun madly out of control as Barbara felt Zack lift her into his arms and carry her across the garden to his room. Still holding her, he closed the French doors and drew the draperies, shutting out the world. The little art-nouveau lamp cast a glow near one corner, but other than that the room lay in shadow and the subdued light of secrets.

He set her on her feet near the huge bed in which he had slept alone for so long, and for a moment Barbara was afraid—not of Zack, not of the physical act of loving him, but of how much of herself she might expose in the act of loving and of how close she had already come to telling him how much she cared.

She lifted her hands to his tie and tugged it loose, then applied her trembling fingers to the gold studs lining his shirtfront. He stood still and silent under her ministrations until she held each of the tiny studs in her hand, then lifted his wrists to her so that she could remove the cuff links, as well. When she had done so, she took one of his hands in hers and placed the jewelry in it. Then she turned and, sweeping her hair to one side with her hand and bending her neck, exposed the button of the halter closure and the tiny zipper hidden in the folds of her dress below her bared back to Zack, for Zack, in an acquiescence and a demand as silent as his had been.

She heard the soft sounds of gold placed on the dark walnut nightstand and felt the tremor in Zack's hands as he released the button, as he slid the zipper down. She caught the top of her dress in her hands and turned toward him, seeing the tension in his taut, beautiful features.

"Love me, Zack," she whispered, releasing the dress and letting it fall to pool at her feet, standing before him in lacy, French-cut tap pants, a wisp of a garter belt and stockings and the jewelry he had given her, as emotionally naked and vulnerable as she was physically. "For tonight, please love me."

He lifted his hand and traced a lingering, tentative pattern across her bared breast. "Always, my darling."

Barbara caught his hand with hers, holding it in place against her sensitized breast, feeling the heat from his fingers work its way through the slight weight he now cupped in his large, gentle hand, as she wanted to hold his words and his love but knew she couldn't.

"No," she said. "Not always. Always can never be for us, Zack. You know that. But tonight is ours and maybe—" She felt her throat clog with unshed tears, with words she could never say, with longings she had hidden and must continue to hide. "And maybe . . . maybe *now* can last for a while longer."

"Barbara . . ."

She didn't know what he saw in her eyes, what she was unable to hide from him, but whatever it was, it silenced him. She felt his hand tense beneath hers and then resume its maddeningly gentle tracing. His features softened and his mouth twisted in a rueful smile.

"I'll never refuse anything you give me, Barbara. Never. But I'll never stop wanting more, either. Or asking for it. Or trying to convince you that you need it, too."

Oh, I do, my darling. I do.

In a perfect world, in a world not touched by hate or fear or pain, she could say that to him. But their world had been touched, had been tainted. And all she had left to give him was the present, was this night, was the way she showed him with her actions and her touch what she must never allow her voice to reveal.

She lifted her hands to his chest, sliding them beneath the edges of his open shirt, gliding them across the light dusting of hair on his smooth, bronzed chest. She felt his breath catch, felt his heartbeat catch and then accelerate, and lifted her face to smile at him—in an invitation that echoed the need she had just felt in his response.

An invitation he answered as he lifted her into his arms and lowered her to the bed, following her. An invitation he answered as his lips and hands reminded her of all she had lost and rekindled in her fires she had once thought she would never again feel, as he lifted her close, so close to ecstasy and then backed away, tantalizing, torturing both of them with the exquisite agony of rising desire, and then returning to drive her even closer to madness.

"Zack..." That was all she was capable of saying—just his name. But in her voice she heard her pleading for release, for... for forever.

He rolled away from her for a moment, and she heard the slide of a drawer, the rip of foil.

"I'd like to pretend to forget this," he said roughly. "To get you pregnant. To tie you with me in any way, in every way that I can. But I can't do that, can I, Barbara?"

She felt tears again building behind her eyes and willed them not to fall. If only he knew. She was already bound to him in every way but the one that would destroy them both. Silently she shook her head, answering the question Zack had already answered for both of them.

Instead she took the package from him, finished opening it, and helped him as he prepared to protect them both. Then she caught his face in her hands and brought it to hers, taking his mouth in a kiss that threatened to devastate her. "Now," she begged. "Oh, please. *Now.*"

And as his body claimed hers, reunited with hers after an eternity of separation, she knew that never again without him would she be whole. And then she knew nothing, be-

cause the release they had both been so long denied over-
took them, throwing them both into a world, a perfect
world, where nothing existed but the two of them in a unity
that their earlier life together, as wonderful as it had been,
had only begun to hint at.

Unbelievably, she slept. Perhaps not long, because in their
sleep, they reached for each other again—once something as
normal to them as the sleep each roused from, now a moment of stolen ecstasy. And as she lay beside him in the af-
terglow of their lovemaking, Barbara wanted to talk with
him of the first time they had made love, of how afraid she
had been then—not of him or the physical expression of
love—of sharing her thoughts, her secrets, her private self
with another person, of giving someone else the power to
hurt her because he did not, could not or would not understand that in spite of having a mind that could compute
wind drag and velocity and understand black holes and
complicated equations, she knew nothing about being a
woman. Nothing about how to give love. How to receive
love.

Until Zack. He had taught her that, lesson by loving lesson.

She couldn't tell him.

But she could store up more memories to treasure: this
sensation of being held protectively in his arms against the
warm length of his strong body, the glow she felt in the aftermath of complete and loving release, the soft kiss of his
breath against her temple, the soft stroking of his hand
through her hair; the silence of the darkened room broken
only by the sounds of their breathing, their heartbeats—the
telephone.

She felt Zack's arm beneath her jerk, then tense at the
first strident ring of the phone, felt that tension spread
quickly through his body as he tightened his hold on her
before reluctantly releasing her and rolling to his other side
to grab the phone.

"What do you have?" he asked without preliminary, as
though he knew who had to be calling.

Barbara watched him withdraw from her with each word of the caller, straightening against the crumpled sheets, sitting up and swinging around to plant his feet firmly on the floor, then standing, pacing within the restrictions of the long cord, unaware of his nudity, unaware of anything but the words he so obviously didn't want to hear.

"I'll be right there," he said. "No. Wait for me. I want to be in on this."

Hanging up the telephone, he glanced at Barbara as he hurried to the antique chest and pulled out jeans and a shirt.

"Zack? What is it?"

He zipped up the jeans, pulled on the shirt and sat on the side of the bed as he tugged on socks and shoes. Only after he was fully dressed did he turn to her and take her in his arms with a desperation that frightened her.

"What is it?" she asked again.

"Nothing," he said. "At least, nothing to worry about. I want you to wait here for me. This won't take long."

"*What* won't take long? Tell me. Please tell me what's happening."

"It's a problem with the computer," he told her. "Something we've been working on for several days."

"A problem with the computer? A problem serious enough to drag you out of bed in the middle of the night. Serious enough for you to hold me as though you thought we'd never see each other again— My God." Her voice broke and when she spoke again it was little more than a whisper. "It's...it's..."

He dropped his hands onto her shoulders, stilling her as she tried to rise. "It's a problem with the computer, Barbara."

She didn't believe him for a minute, but she sank back down on the bed, letting him think she did.

"Wait here for me?" he said again.

She nodded and he pulled her into his arms for another quick but equally desperate embrace before hurrying from the room.

Suddenly chilled, Barbara pushed herself up against the headboard, taking the sheet with her, until she sat huddled in a tented cocoon, knees up almost beneath her chin, and stared out over the shadows of the room.

The similarity between this and another time tugged at the edge of her consciousness until she searched her memory and found another time, a lifetime before, when she had sat alone in a strange room—a time when she had promised she would rebuild her life, that she would find her way out of the nightmare her life had become.

A lifetime before.

And the nightmare continued.

And now Zack was trapped in it, too. Again? Still?

She whimpered and tugged the sheet closer.

Wait here? While he went off to face God only knew what? While she gave in to weakness and fear of the unknown threat? She didn't think so.

She threw off the sheet and stood, scrambling into Zack's robe for the trip down the hall. Whatever threatened Zack also threatened her. And whatever it was, she wouldn't let it find her hiding under the covers.

When Zack reached the foyer, he found the elevator door closed and two guards instead of the usual one. He nodded his approval. "Mr. Adams asks that you use the stairs," one of the men told him. "We have two men there, too. No one will get on this floor."

Grim-faced but somewhat reassured, Zack nodded again as he turned and strode toward the back stairs. A guard stepped away from the door when he saw him approaching, and Zack nodded at the man, pausing only long enough to key in the proper code before he hurried into the stairwell.

Taylor Adams and Jamie waited for him at the stairwell entrance on the floor below. Both of them looked as if they had also been roused from bed. He found a wry smile for his usually meticulously groomed security chief in spite of the seriousness of the moment, but quickly became all business.

"Where is he?" he asked. "Somewhere on the upper floors, I assume, since you didn't want the noise of the elevator."

Taylor nodded, but led Zack through the reception rooms to the outer hallway where another half dozen of Taylor's privately recruited security force waited before speaking. "He's at your terminal again."

Zack's mouth tightened. "How did he get up here? And what's he doing?"

"We don't know," Taylor told him, equally as grim. "Our first indication was the warning we had programmed into the computer to alert us. No one saw him come into the building. None of our cameras picked him up in any elevator, stairwell, or hallway. He breached the passwords, browsed through files for a while, and then we lost track of him, but he's still in there. Somewhere."

"What? That's not possible."

"Maybe not, Zack," Jamie said. "But someone is still logged in to the mainframe and in spite of all of our fail safes, we haven't a clue as to what he's looking at or doing."

"Then let's find out," Zack said.

"*We'll* find out," Adams told him. "You stay here."

"Like hell I will. It's my life he's playing with, and I'm tired of it. I'm so damn tired of it."

Taylor nodded once and opened the door to Zack's reception area. Zack went immediately to the receptionist's desk and reached for the intercom. "I've been programming this each night," he said. "I thought it might come in handy." He flipped a switch and the gathered men listened to the sounds from his office coming through the tiny speaker. Silence. Except for the rhythmic, sliding sound of paper through his laser printer. Zack turned off the speaker and looked at Taylor.

"He's printing his work?" Taylor whispered incredulously.

"Sounds like it," Jamie answered, also in a whisper. "But why? Why doesn't he just copy it to disk or use the modem to export it to another computer? He's done everything else, so I know none of our blocks would stop him if he wanted to."

Zack looked at the men around him and then at the door to his office. "Why don't we ask him?"

Taylor nodded and drew his automatic from the shoulder holster he wore over his shirt. Jamie nodded and drew a .38 revolver from the holster he wore at the back of his belt. The other men, also armed, nodded and drew their weapons. Zack accepted the need for armed guards—his life had made denying that need foolhardy and dangerous—but he had never grown comfortable with such blatant use of personal protection. And when they arrived at his office door and Taylor reached for the doorknob, Zack realized that he probably never would.

He put his hand on the doorknob. "My office," he said softly. "My problem, and my life. I go first."

"We go together," Taylor insisted, raising his arm and his weapon in preparation for that entrance.

Zack nodded, swallowed once, and faced the doorway. Was he afraid? Or was he finally so angry that he had no room for fear? Whatever the emotion that raged through his body, he knew he had to vent it in some way. "Try not to shoot me by mistake," he said to the men behind him. He heard a nervous laugh someone tried to turn into a cough. He tightened his hand on the doorknob and felt the mechanism slide silently.

"All right," he said. "Let's go."

"Freeze!" he heard Taylor shout from beside him as he thrust open the door and he and eight armed men crowded into his office.

But they were the ones who froze when they saw the intruder sitting at Zack's terminal and reflected in the mirror on the wall behind it. For a moment Zack's mind was unable to comprehend the whole picture, only fragmented portions of it: hands raising hesitantly toward the ceiling, eyes wide with surprise and startled fear, riotous short red curls, hot-pink pajamas with feet in them, and holding on her lap an overweight and highly contented cat.

"Mickie?" Zack choked out, breaking the silence that for several seconds had been broken only by the restrained noises of his laser printer.

"Wow," she answered, her eyes growing even larger and brighter. "Wow."

She was gone. *Oh, God!* Barbara caught her hand to her mouth to choke back her anguished cry. While she had made love with Zack, while she had lain with him with no thoughts than for the two of them, her daughter had disappeared.

Barbara tried to convince herself that nothing was wrong, that Mickie was just somewhere in this oversize apartment, but Zack's mysterious telephone call and middle-of-the-night mission told her that she would be stretching coincidence much too tightly if she convinced herself of Mickie's safety. Still, she peeked into Dianne's room to make sure Mickie wasn't there, even opened the door to Meg's office to make sure Mickie wasn't caught up in some computer game, before she allowed her panic to overwhelm her and she ran to the foyer, to the guard posted there, and found two men at attention instead of the usual one who always before had seemed preoccupied with other work.

A computer problem? Oh, no. Whatever had summoned him was more. Much more. Wilson Truett? Of course, it had to be. And had Zack known that now that monster had her daughter?

"Find Zack," she sobbed, unable to say more, unable to explain.

One of the guards pressed at his ear, and Barbara noticed the wiring of an earpiece. "They're on their way upstairs, now," the guard told her. "Everything's all right."

No, it wasn't, Barbara thought. And it wouldn't be until she held her daughter in her arms and saw with her own eyes that both Mickie and Zack were safe.

She heard the rumble of the elevator then and looked up as the doors opened. Zack and Taylor... and, thank God, Mickie, stepped out. Mickie's new pink pajamas had a streak of dirt the length of one leg, and she clutched Taylor's hand, a clear sign that she was pretty sure she was in trouble. Taylor's hand, not Zack's. But Barbara couldn't stop to sort that out, not now.

"Mickie," she said, biting back a sob as she dropped to her knees and clutched her daughter to her. "You're all right," she said, burying her face in her daughter's curls. "You're all right."

Not releasing Mickie—she couldn't bear to do that yet—she looked up at Zack. "How did he get her? Is she really all right? Did you catch him? Why didn't you tell me she was in danger?"

Zack shook his head and, as though not knowing what else to do, he glanced at the stack of papers he held in one hand. "It was a false alarm," he said.

"A false alarm? You left here in the middle of the night and came back with my daughter and you tell me it was a false alarm?"

"Barbara—" Taylor began, but Zack interrupted him with a quick, slicing gesture.

"You'd better see about that other matter, Taylor."

Taylor nodded and left the foyer.

"Let's get her back in bed and then we can talk, Barbara," Zack said, taking Barbara's arm and lifting her to her feet. "Mickie is all right. I promise you that."

Barbara looked at the two guards remaining in the hall before sighing and nodding to Zack, scooping Mickie up into her arms and turning toward the hall.

Zack followed her to Mickie's room and waited silently while she got clean pajamas from the drawer and sent Mickie into the bath to change.

"Now," she said. "Tell me what happened."

Leaning back against the door facing, Zack closed his eyes and sighed. "We've had a burglar," he said. "A computer thief. And no matter how careful we were, we couldn't seem to catch this...this intruder in the act. Until tonight."

"But how did Mickie get involved?" Barbara asked. "How did he get his hands on her?"

"Barbara," Zack said slowly, opening his eyes at last and looking into hers. "Mickie is the intruder."

"What?"

Zack thrust the stack of papers he still held toward her. "And this is what she was doing."

Barbara took the papers and glanced at them. "A book?"

"Not just any book, apparently," Zack said. "Look at the illustrations."

Barbara sorted through the pages unable to believe what Zack had just told her, that her daughter had circumvented his security system, had broken into a computer she knew to be almost impenetrable, to write a picture book. She glanced at the pictures of the mother and father, and then peered sharply at them. Her face and Zack's. And the child? She studied it, but other than red hair she found nothing familiar. She looked up at Zack just as the bathroom door opened and Mickie came back into the room. Mickie studied them for a moment and then silently climbed into her bed and pulled the sheet up to her chin.

"Mickie..." Barbara said, but a heavy thud at the window silenced her. She twisted around to see Tesla sitting warily on the window ledge.

"Damn!" Zack said softly. "I've got four men plugging the holes and that creature managed to elude all of them and get back—"

"It's not his fault," Mickie cried, breaking her silence. "I just followed him. Don't get rid of him, Zack. Please? Please!"

Zack shook his head and walked to the window, plucking the cat from his perch and chucking him under the chin. "You old reprobate," he said. "You're going to get all of us in trouble one of these days."

He walked to the bed and released Tesla to hop down beside Mickie. "Of course I'm not going to get rid of him," he said.

Mickie scooped Tesla into her arms and buried her face in his fur.

"You followed him?" Barbara asked, not sure she wanted an answer. "Where?"

"Through the air-conditioner vents," Mickie mumbled.

"Where?"

"The air-conditioner vents. One of them comes out in a little room behind Zack's office."

"It was always my terminal reflected in the log," Zack told her. "But there was never any physical evidence of anyone getting upstairs."

"Mickie, do you know that if you had gotten in the wrong vent, you could have fallen all the way to the basement? That you could have been... That you could have been lost in those pipes and we wouldn't have known where to look for you. That—"

"Mo-om. I didn't. And I knew what I was doing, honest."

Zack sighed. Again. And realized he had been doing a lot of that since they had burst in on an intrepid and highly ingenious burglar and found this imp. He ought to be angry, damn angry, but somehow he just couldn't summon the anger. "And what were you doing in the computer those times that you blocked our trackers? Have you done some damage there that we're not going to discover until we're involved in something up to our necks?"

Mickie echoed his sigh. "I didn't hurt anything. I just didn't want anyone to know I'd been in the files. Some people get really upset about that. And I was working on something I didn't want anyone else to know about, so I hid the files. That's all."

"That's all," Zack repeated, incredulous.

"What were you working on, Mickie?" Barbara asked. "No. No, no, no. The question is, What were you *thinking* of, Mickie? You know I've warned you about your explorations. I told you that we can't repay Zack's hospitality by infringing on his privacy. What made you think his computer or his office was any different from his room or the personal things he keeps there?''

"But, Mom, it's really neat. I knew you had worked for Zack—I mean, I heard someone say you had once worked here, so I wanted to see if I could find anything you'd worked on, and then I wanted to do this story, so I went back into the personnel files and got your picture and Zack's for my people, and I wanted to get one of me to use but Zack didn't have one in the computer, but he's got these really neat videos of us and I was trying to figure out how to get my picture off the video and into the computer with the hardware he's got there, and I've almost got it figured out but I need a scanner or some patch cords before I can check out the program, and..."

Zack knew the moment the importance of Mickie's innocent revelations penetrated Barbara's consciousness. He saw her stiffen, saw the color drain from her already pale face, saw her hands tighten on the pages she held.

She handed the pages to him, not even waiting to see if he took them before she bent to her daughter and covered child and cat both with the light blanket from the foot of the bed.

"Shh," she said. "We've all had enough excitement for tonight. But I'm going to talk with you again about this tomorrow, and the day after, and the day after that if I think it's necessary. You've got to learn there are things you shouldn't do even if you think you are able to. Now, go to sleep. And yes, I love you."

She waited only until she had closed the door to Mickie's room behind them to turn to him. "Videos?" she asked. "Do I want to see them?"

Zack braced his hand against the wall, blocking her should she try to flee, wanting to block out the pain this new revelation must bring her. But he couldn't. "Maybe you should," he said finally. "Maybe if you can tell us when and where they were taken, we'll be able to come up with some kind of lead, because God knows, up until now all we've followed have led to dead ends."

"When...and where?"

He thought for a moment she would faint, and caught her in his arms to keep her from falling.

"I—I had hoped these were videos you had had taken," she said in little more than a whisper. "Maybe I'd better see them. Maybe...maybe I'd better learn just how long I've been lying to myself about being safe."

Eight

Nothing in Zachary's new office reminded her of the one that had once been familiar to her. Almost nothing, Barbara amended. On his desk sat one reminder of happier days, a paperweight she had given him—a small pewter replica of an old movie-studio logo: an out-of-scale but still very tiny single-engine airplane circling the earth.

Barbara drew in her breath when she saw the paperweight but refused to let herself speak. He had kept the strangest assortment of things—an inexpensive paperweight, a worthless cat, a whimsical lamp and an armoire that wouldn't fit in any normal-ceilinged room.

And she recognized the common thread that tied them all together. All had been either her gift to him or his to her. *Oh, Zack, why couldn't you have forgotten me? You were supposed to put me out of your mind, not hold on to the memories.*

And, of course, the topaz earrings and her rings.

She had put the earrings back in their jeweler's box when she'd gone to her room to dress, but the rings—the rings she had put on for "just a few minutes" earlier tonight—she still wore. Realizing that, she once again clasped her left hand in her right.

The offices blazed with light, and from an open door at one end of Zack's private domain, she heard noises, hammering, a scraping sound, a subdued oath, before the light in that room switched off and Jamie Jameson, unkempt, disheveled, wearing his weapon but carrying a toolbox, emerged from that room. He stopped, his surprise at seeing her downstairs evident on his pleasant, wholesome face, and nodded in acknowledgment of her presence.

"Mrs. Gordon." He grinned at her, all pretense of formality gone. "That's some kid you've got yourself. For a while I actually thought I was keeping up with her."

Barbara returned his smile. "Thank you, Jamie," she said, for his words had been complimentary. "Sometimes I fool myself into thinking I'm keeping up with her, too."

Jamie looked at Zack, held up his toolbox and shrugged. "The grate's secure, now," he said. "But the cat has disappeared again."

"I know," Zack told him. "He's upstairs."

"Do you want me to—?"

Zack shook his head. "No. Leave him where he is tonight. We'll find time to worry about his sleeping arrangements tomorrow."

Barbara saw Zack drop all pretense of hiding his tension when he closed his office door behind Jamie and turned to face her. He waved her toward a leather-covered chair in front of his desk and crossed to the television and videocassette recorder set up across the room.

Not turning to face her, he pulled cassettes from the cabinet and stacked them on top of the television.

"I'll play these in the order they arrived," he said, his voice calm, so calm, but he slammed the tape into the machine.

She watched silently until she saw herself pick up the newspaper, frown, and scan the neighborhood with a wary glance.

"I thought it was my imagination," she said, more to herself than to Zack.

She watched, silent again after that, the backward progression in time, the scenes of herself and her daughter caught in moments that should have been shared with Zack, that in the perfect world she often grieved *would* have been shared with him, that almost every day of her life she had wanted to share with him, until the footage of her and Mickie at the bakery and in the park.

"Her fifth birthday," she said. Drawing a watery breath, she brushed at her cheeks.

"When?" Zack asked, still facing the TV, his back to her.

"March 18."

He nodded, not saying anything else until he rewound the tape and inserted another.

"This is the last of them. It arrived this—yesterday morning, now. I don't know why the time jump."

Barbara watched herself carrying a three-year-old Mickie, walking beside Meg, who pushed Dianne in a wheelchair, toward the complex that housed Texas Children's Hospital.

"It's right after we arrived in Houston, the reason why we came. We're taking Dianne in for another—for her last surgery, so far."

The second scene flashed onto the screen, and Barbara caught her hand to her mouth to hold back a cry. "And that's—" She stared in horror at the pleasant, two-story frame house. "That's— We lived there for a year before we moved to Houston."

Zack switched off the set and turned at last to face her. She felt his caress on her wet cheeks as plainly as though he had physically touched her, but he made no move to cross the room.

"Tell me what happened after you left," he said. "Where you went, what you did. How you survived."

Make me understand why you left.

She heard those words, too, although he hadn't spoken them, as clearly as she had felt him not touch her.

She nodded. "I—you knew I closed out my personal checking account?"

"Yes. We traced you as far as the bank. But no farther."

"I caught a bus," she said. "I didn't know where I was going, and the bus company was having one of those promotions they used to have. I bought a two-week pass and just rode, getting off the bus when I felt like it, sometimes sleeping on it. Eventually, I wound up in a little town in northern Louisiana.

"Meg lived there, actually a few miles outside of town in a house that had belonged to her husband's family. I saw her ad for a live-in housekeeper weeks after I arrived, and after I knew I—I knew I was pregnant. I didn't think she was going to hire me—she didn't until a few days later. She's been more than an employer, she's been a true friend. I don't know what I would have done without her, or the job...."

"You could have come back to me. I would have given my life to keep you safe."

This time she couldn't hold back her sob. "I know." She'd always known that. And Wilson Truett knew it, too.

Zack turned toward the wall of windows. The draperies were open; the sky the light gray of early morning. "March 18," he said finally. "She's really too young to have started first grade then, isn't she?"

Barbara nodded in one quick, jerky move. "Yes. She's in private school with Dianne. Meg paid her tuition, partly as a bonus for me, partly because she is so good with Dianne. She started kindergarten this fall, and they—the school—promoted her to first without—without telling me until it was already done. I don't know what I would have said had they asked—probably, I would have refused. I want her to grow up with children her own age. I want her to have the companionship, the friendship, I missed out on. But I want her to enjoy learning, too."

"March 18."

"Zack, don't do this."

"She could be my—our daughter."

"I know."

Zack whirled to face her and slammed his fist down on a nearby table. "Damn him! Why? *Why?*"

"Because he's a sick man. He doesn't need a reason for doing what he does. If he ever had one, he's probably forgotten what it was. He hates, Zack. And his hatred may be focused on you, but it goes beyond you."

"How can you be so understanding?"

"How can I not be, unless I want to wind up as warped and twisted as he is?"

"Barbara—"

She stood, knowing she had to end this conversation, knowing she had to leave Zack—this moment, and, eventually, completely. "Don't be too angry with Mickie, Zack. I'll talk to her about her forays into your computer. And I'll find some way to explain about the videos—I'll have to. But I will do my best to see that she doesn't intrude on your life too much."

"Barbara."

She allowed herself to look at him, then and saw the naked agony in his eyes.

"I love you."

She took one deep breath, willing herself not to break under the wave of pain she felt coming from him, a pain she knew only too intimately. "I know."

Zack had let her leave then. She walked dry-eyed to the elevator, found it waiting with the doors standing open, pushed the panel for the penthouse, and rode upstairs. The two guards still waited in the foyer. She passed them without speaking and went to Mickie's room.

Mickie had kicked off the blanket and lay sprawled across the bed with Tesla curled at her side. Barbara stood watching her for several minutes, her thoughts spinning out of control—from what she had to tell her daughter to what she really wanted for her, for all of them, and knew they couldn't have. Finally, though, she acknowledged her exhaustion. Slipping off her shoes, she slid into bed with Mickie, pulled the blanket up over her, Mickie, and the cat, and took Mickie into her arms.

"Hmpff?"

"Hush, darling," Barbara whispered. "Sleep. Just sleep."

Mickie responded to her quiet voice and snuggled close to her. And as Barbara held her precious weight against her, as she nuzzled her face into her daughter's baby-fine, sweet-smelling curls, she at last gave in to the pain she shared with Zack, gave in to the tears that she had tried so hard to keep from falling, gave in to the desperation that had gripped her, followed her, haunted her for so long. "Zack," she whispered. "Oh, Zack. What can I do? *What can I do?*"

Nothing. She could do nothing. But wait. As Zack waited. For Wilson Truett to make some careless move and thus release them.

Barbara spoke to Mickie the next day about the danger she had been in while wandering around in air-conditioning vents, about the impropriety of stealing into Zack's office and his computer without permission, even about her lack of real regret for her actions.

Mickie apologized to Zack, but she remained quiet, subdued, almost sullen for two days until Jamie and two more of Taylor's men delivered an assortment of boxes to Mickie's room and unpacked a personal computer more powerful than the university mainframe on which Barbara had trained and every peripheral attachment known to electronic wizardry, including a modem and a private telephone line to access no fewer than three information services.

"It's too much," Barbara told Jamie. "It's almost as though he's rewarding her for being a successful burglar."

He grinned and kept on installing the equipment. "Mr. Gordon had ordered a computer for the girls before we discovered how talented Mickie really is. She would have had the computer even if she had never followed the cat. But—" he chuckled and popped another disk into the drive to install it "—I will admit this setup is a little more sophisticated than he had first imagined."

"Does he know just how sophisticated?"

Jamie nodded. "He knows. In fact, he was the one who came to me and admitted that perhaps he had underestimated the girls' needs."

* * *

She spoke also to Meg, seeking her out as she sat in her office in front of a computer screen that carried no more copy than it had days before. She approached the subjects carefully, but she had to talk to Meg about the writer's block that still gripped her friend, about her uncharacteristic actions the last time they'd spoken.

"I'm sorry, Barbara. I shouldn't have snapped at you. But it really isn't your fault."

"No? I know you scheduled Dianne's surgeries and your contracts as well as you could so that you could take time off from your writing. But there were times when you couldn't do that. And not even then did you stay blocked as long as you have since Zack found us."

Meg looked back at the screen, sighed, and then fumbled through a stack of mail on her desk, finally pulling out the envelope Barbara had once casually identified as an invitation.

"Maybe this will help," Meg said. "I'd forgotten this conference, but I've promised to speak at it. Maybe the change of pace will be good for me. That is, if Zack will let me go."

"You're not a prisoner here, Meg."

Meg smiled wanly. "Aren't I, Barbara? Aren't we all?"

So, at last, she could no longer put off speaking to Zack. Except for brief, frustrating moments at meals when he continued to act toward her as he had begun acting the day before their ill-fated dinner, she hadn't spoken to him since viewing the tapes. She hadn't known what to say to him that hadn't already been said. She didn't know now what to say to him. But she did know she had to plead for Meg.

She waited until after dinner, waited until after she had heard him in the pool, waited, this time, until he had time to shower and change, and then, choosing the slightly more formal approach of the hallway, she went to his room.

He opened the door only moments after she knocked. And he was fully dressed, which Barbara knew could mean only that he would again be doing whatever he and Taylor did in the dark hours of night to track down and trap Truett.

Don't let him be hurt, she pleaded silently. *Oh, please, don't let him be hurt.*

His eyes reflected his surprise at seeing her at his door before quickly masking it, but his posture and the implacable set of his features revealed to her all too clearly his wariness at her appearance.

She fought a brief flare of anger at his reaction. She was the one who should be wary of him. She never knew when he was going to drop a hand on her shoulder, a kiss on her lips, or grab her in a quick hug, regardless of who was present to witness it. While she—

She felt the color rising in her cheeks at the thought of the hours she had spent with him in this room and schooled her features as carefully as he had his. He was right to be wary, she thought. He had no way of knowing whether she approached him this time with a demand for her freedom or a plea for him to take her to bed.

"I need to speak with you for only a few minutes. I thought it would be better to do it now rather than interrupt you in your office."

There, she thought carefully. She had let him know by her words and attitude that this was a—well, almost—a business call, not a personal one.

Of course it was a personal one. Everything between them was personal, had to be personal, would be personal to the end of time. No matter how she had tried to change that. No matter how hard she continued to try.

He stepped back, holding the door open for her. "Come in."

She shook her head. "No. This won't take but a moment—"

Abruptly he took her hand and tugged her into the room, closing the door behind her. Just as abruptly he crossed the room to the table where the art-nouveau lamp glowed softly and began straightening a stack of papers and stashing them in a leather portfolio.

"Well?" he asked, closing the case and at last turning to face her.

"It's— I've come about Meg."

She watched as he slumped slightly and then regained his almost militarily erect posture. "Of course," he said. "Anything or anyone but yourself."

"Zack—"

He shook his head in an angry, gruff gesture. "Never mind. I suppose the tension of the last few weeks has finally caught up with me."

"Has it, now?" Barbara couldn't believe she had spoken the words. But he wasn't the only one fighting tension. And *she* wasn't the only one sending out mixed signals. Suddenly all the emotions that had roiled and churned within her for longer than she could remember found an expression—anger—and fair or not, warranted or not, justified or not, an outlet—Zack. "It doesn't seem to be bothering you at mealtimes, when you appear to be doing your best to convince everyone around us that we're living the lives of Ward and June Cleaver."

Zack threw the portfolio onto the chair. "How do you want me to act, Barbara? Tell me. Is there a code of etiquette for this situation? Are there rules to follow? If there are, for God's sake, clue me in on what they are."

"I don't know!" she cried. "But you can't go on acting as though nothing has happened!"

"No. I can't, can I?" he said in a voice chilling in its quiet control.

"Zack?"

He crossed the room and captured her face in his hands, cradling it, holding her still. "And that's what I've been trying to do. Pretending that nothing had separated us. Pretending that nothing threatened you or me. Pretending that our life could go on just the way it had before we were separated. Pretending that if I just gave you enough time to get used to me, to this apartment, to the way we have to live now, that everything would be the same as it had been. But pretending does no good, does it, Barbara? And waiting does no good."

For a moment, she was afraid of Zachary Gordon. For a moment, the intensity of his voice, in his words, in his touch, brought forth insecurities she thought she had long ago dealt with. For a moment, tears and sobs caught in her throat, holding her silent, holding her still.

"You love me," he said, and his hands speared into her hair, tilting her face up to his, "but you won't tell me in words, and if you're ever weak enough to show me your love in your actions, you back away as though our love is something shameful.

"And I love you. But you don't want me to. Except, maybe, on some physical level.

"But that's not enough, Barbara. I need your love. I need to know that you understand that our love was not what has caused all our pain. I need your trust. I need to know that you know I'll never let any harm come to you again. I need the words, I need the actions, I need the sharing, I need..."

His words faded as he bent toward her, as his mouth claimed hers in a devastating act of possession, as his hands finally released her hair to go around her, to lift her against him with strength and determination in a sensual onslaught as devastating, as possessive, as his kiss.

And as her anger had fired his anger, Zack's passion fired Barbara's. She lifted her arms to his shoulders, holding on to him as she tried to get even closer in this awkward embrace, as her mouth opened beneath his, as she met his aggression with a hungry aggression of her own, until he turned, bracing her against the door, and she felt the heat and strength of his arousal against her belly.

She moaned, unable to deny her need for him, unable to hide anything he wanted to see in her eyes or in her actions.

She felt the unexpected knock on the door behind her, felt Zack stiffen.

"Zack?" Taylor Adams's voice sounded clearly through the closed door. "You wanted to see me?"

"Damn!" Zack whispered as Barbara felt the passion drain from her, leaving her limp and feeling vulnerable and exposed as he continued to hold her against himself.

"I'll be a few minutes, Taylor," Zack said, and Barbara wondered if Taylor could hear the thickening of Zack's voice, the labored breathing. "Wait for me by the pool."

"Right."

She heard no sounds as he walked away from the room, but then, no one could have. The thick carpet masked his exit as much as it had masked his arrival. But she doubted she would have heard the arrival of the proverbial herd of elephants.

Slowly, Zack loosened his grasp on her and lowered her until her feet touched the floor, but he didn't release her. He dropped his head until his forehead rested against hers.

"I've wanted to do that since Taylor first brought me word he'd found you," he said through tortured breaths. "Not chaste kisses, not restrained touches, not even, as wonderful as it was, the gentle love we shared the one night. But *this*. Unrestrained. Uninhibited. *Honest.*"

Barbara let herself remain yielding in his arms. *Unrestrained and uninhibited?* Yes. Their kiss had been all of that. So much so that had they not been interrupted she might have dragged Zack down to the Kirman rug that covered almost half the carpet in his bedroom and made equally unrestrained and uninhibited love with him.

But honest?

As much as she wanted Zack, right this moment and for the rest of her life, she had not been and could not be honest with him. Not for her sake, his sake, or Mickie's. And why was she finding it so necessary to keep reminding herself of that indisputable truth?

Almost as though he sensed her emotional withdrawal from him, Zack released her. He stepped back, smoothing his hands through his hair, retucking his shirt, turning away from her.

"But that's not why you came to me tonight, is it?" he asked.

"No. I—"

"Meg," he reminded her gently, seeming, once again, to be in complete control of himself. His lips even curved in a rueful smile. "You came to talk to me about some problem with Meg."

"I— Yes. About Meg."

He walked to her and with a gentle hand under her chin, lifted her face to his, once again the careful and considerate Zack he had been since he'd found her. But in the rich darkness of his eyes, she saw a glimmer of the other Zack, the Zack whose passions lay too close to the surface, the Zack who could ignite her with only a touch.

"Tomorrow," he said softly, releasing her from his touch but not from the spell his eyes continued to cast. "I'll make time for us after breakfast tomorrow." Again his beautiful sculptured lips lifted in a rueful smile. "And maybe by then we'll even be able to think about her. And her problem."

He turned away from her and walked back to his reading chair, where he picked up the leather portfolio. "Taylor will be looking for me if I don't meet him soon, and while I could cancel this meeting, I don't think you want him speculating about why I did so."

She said nothing, only stepped away from the door so that he could open it when he again reached her side.

"Go to bed, Barbara," he told her, still in the same quiet voice. "It's late. Both of us are running on adrenaline and emotions. We don't need to say anything else tonight. Anything that would... that would drive us farther apart than we already are."

Was that what he thought she had meant to do? She met his steady glance with one of her own, hiding the truth she could deny from him, if not from herself. Yes. That was exactly what she had meant to do.

She swallowed back her words and her agony that they were necessary and leaned forward slightly, allowing herself the small luxury of leaning against his strength for these few seconds.

And there was one other thing she couldn't hide from him. Her fear for his safety. "Be careful, Zack," she said softly. "Whatever you and Taylor do, please be careful."

Nine

———

"**I** don't think it's safe," Taylor said.

"I'm not absolutely sure it is, either," Zack admitted, walking around his desk to the wall of windows and looking out over the Houston skyline. It was the middle of the morning. Their one semisubstantial lead had failed to materialize. No further tapes had arrived from Truett. All the talent at their disposal had failed to find anything else to go on.

Nothing, in fact, had happened, except an extremely unsatisfactory discussion with Barbara that morning after breakfast—a discussion held in sight, if not within hearing range, of members of his staff.

Zack recognized her defensive tactic in insisting that they speak in the breakfast room. He couldn't blame her for not wanting to be alone with him after his caveman tactics of the night before. Yes. He could. Because she had responded to him; impossible as it now seemed, she had wanted him as much as he had wanted her.

But once again she was hiding from him behind a wall of reserve that, for now at least, seemed impenetrable—a wall he knew too well had been built by fear. A wall he wondered if he had any right to even attempt to destroy.

"Zack?"

Zack shook his head. "Sorry. I—"

"You had other things on your mind."

"Yes. Yes, I did."

"Should I come back later?"

"No." Zack turned away from the midmorning glare. "Barbara wants this. Meg wants it. Barbara wasn't particularly gentle in telling me Meg thinks we've got her in some kind of prison. And she wasn't particularly gentle in reminding me how much she owes Meg Riley. She also seems to think—and I believe I agree with her—that Truett has no interest in Meg."

"But we can't just let her go waltzing off to a conference in Phoenix. My God, what if we're wrong?"

"She's not writing. Did you know that, Taylor?"

At Taylor's frown, Zack nodded. "I wondered if she'd told you."

"Why should she tell me anything?"

"Taylor, Taylor. I am not blind. There's an attraction between the two of you, and yes, it does run both ways. Meg has contractual obligations to fulfill, and one of those is a speaking engagement at a writers' conference in Phoenix. Do we keep her here, against her will, and possibly do serious damage to her career because she is too strung out to do what she obviously has been able to do quite well in the past, in spite of serious obstacles? Or do we minimize the risk and let her go? I don't think we have any choice."

"And just how do we minimize the risk?"

For the first time that morning, Zack allowed himself to smile. "By sending you with her, of course."

Taylor smiled, too, a conspirator's satisfied grin, but soon sobered. "You know I can't go off and leave you unprotected—"

"Unprotected? In a high rise with every electronic security gadget known to man? With more security personnel than some police forces? It's only for three days, Taylor. Because of all the times she has helped Barbara, I owe Meg much more than this trip, but right now, this is all I can do for her."

Zack took a folded paper out of his pocket and handed it to Taylor. "These are the details of the conference. Have your staff make any arrangements you think necessary."

Taylor hadn't been easy to convince, even though he had wanted to be convinced that going to Phoenix with Meg Riley was the prudent and correct thing to do. That it was also something he very much wanted to do didn't escape Zack's attention, but neither did it make his job of convincing Taylor to abandon what he considered his primary duty any easier.

His highly efficient staff, aware that he was under some unusual tension but, with the exception of Taylor's crew, not knowing what that tension was, functioned at peak performance, so after his conference with Taylor, Zack found little but routine chores to divert his attention from the major problem—*problems*—of his life. Those that waited for him upstairs. Those that he had no earthly idea how to resolve.

Zack gave up the pretense of trying to work in midafternoon and returned to the penthouse. The reception areas were quiet and empty, except for the security agent in the foyer who nodded at him as he stepped out of the elevator.

Rather than take the risk of running into anyone by going through the apartment, Zack cut through to the garden, intent on making his way to his room and some necessary solitude so that he could work on the problem of how to reach Barbara. But as he approached the pool, he came to a sudden stop as he heard the sounds from behind the foliage: a light plunk, a soft whirring noise, a quiet scuffle of clothes and shoes, the whirring noise and the plunk again, and finally, a childish mutter.

Mickie?

Zack debated returning to his offices before she realized he was there. He had seen her at meals, but she had spoken

to him directly only twice since the debacle in his office:
once, very subdued, as she gave him an obviously re-
hearsed apology, and once, with almost normal exuber-
ance, as she thanked him for the computer.

He didn't know what to say to her. He thought perhaps
he ought to be angry at the merry chase she had led all of
them on as she played with unconcerned abandon in a
highly sensitive, intruder-proofed computer system. But
when he thought of the frustration of the best security people available in the private sector when not only could they
not stop the intrusion, they couldn't even track her as she
built her picture book and played her games, Zack knew he
couldn't be angry with her. What he could do was picture
her as he had first seen her, wearing a neon pink nightshirt
and ordering both him and Taylor with every assurance that
she would be obeyed, and as she had appeared that night,
again in pink, with her hands in the air and her eyes wide—
not with fear but with excitement—as a horde of armed men
burst into the room to apprehend her.

No. He couldn't be angry.

And he couldn't continue to avoid her.

But facing her also meant facing the pain that so far he
had managed to keep to a dull, gnawing roar.

This was the child that should have been his. His to nur-
ture, to love, to watch grow, to share with his wife in laughter and in love.

And this was the child that his stepbrother had taken away
from him, had used to taunt him with pictures of the life
Zack should have been part of. Had used to drive another
wedge between Zack and Barbara.

Had used.

Zack felt the blow to his conscience, clean but not killing, as he recognized a truth he had not let himself consider. Wilson had used a child in his senseless, heartless
vendetta against Zack. And Zack had let him. In his pain,
in his grief, he had recognized the child only as a weapon,
not as an innocent who was as much a victim as her mother
had been. *Oh, God,* Zack thought. *How could I have let*

myself do that? And then, with equally brutal clarity, he wondered, *Does she know?*

Of course she suspected something—if there was anything this child of Barbara's was not, it was insensitive—but she couldn't possibly have enough facts to know *why* he had acted toward her as he had. And if he had any acting talent whatsoever, she never would know, Zack swore.

The whirring and plunking had continued on the other side of the foliage, and by now the childish mutters had grown louder and more grumbling.

He ought to leave. Ought to back away before she knew he was there. Ought to go through the house and take the risk of running into Barbara, or return to his office. Anything but stand there like an awkward spy, held transfixed in place by a six-year-old child.

But then she spoke.

"Oh, rat feathers!"

Rat feathers? Zack felt a reluctant smile at the oath. Whatever that whirring and plunking was all about had one very bright little girl very perturbed.

Her grumbling increased, he heard something—inanimate and small, definitely not Mickie—hit the surface of the pool, and as he heard the whirring and plunking resume, Zack felt a glimmer of recognition at the sounds. Intrigued, knowing he had to be wrong about the cause of the sounds, but also knowing he had to take this opportunity to visit with the child, to try to bridge the awkwardness between them that he had caused, Zack took a few steps to bypass the foliage and reach poolside.

And he hadn't been wrong about the noises.

He shook his head, giving his smile its freedom. The slap of an object against the water had been caused by a small inflatable ring; the whirring and plunking by a fine example of a fly rod and reel and a lightweight, probably hand-tied fly hitting the water. The grumbling was self-explanatory. Mickie. Who seemed to be getting the fly closer to the ring each time but couldn't quite cast the fly into the ring.

Mickie reeled in her line and turned toward an open book perched on the wrought-iron table beside her, studied the pages, and then turned back toward the pool with a determined scowl twisting her mouth before she saw Zack standing nearby.

Her scowl faded as she watched him warily.

"Hi, Mickie."

"'Lo, Zack," she mumbled.

"Catching anything?"

"Course not," she said indignantly. "You know there aren't any fish in this pool." She must have decided his smile was genuine, because she grinned at him. "But there are in that little one by your room. Maybe when I get a little better with this thing, I'll try it over there."

"May I try?" he asked.

He saw her surprise, but she quickly finished reeling in the last few feet of the line and handed him the rod.

"Nice rig," Zack said, testing the weight of it and finding it just about perfect for her small size, testing the tension of the line and finding it just about perfect, period.

"Thanks. Tewkie bought it for me to practice with."

"Tewkie?"

"Mr. Tewksbury, the guard at the elevator."

Tewksbury, the ex-special forces officer. Zack shuddered to think what would have happened to him if he had called the man "Tewkie."

"It's all in the wrist, you see," Zack told her, easing out a length of line and deftly flicking it so that the fly landed within the ring.

Mickie looked at him with new appreciation, and he again flicked the line, freeing the fly from the ring and reeling it in. "That's what the book says. That's what Tewkie said, too. The problem is, nobody says *what* it is that's in the wrist, or *how* it's in there, or how *I'm* supposed to get it out. Can you do that again?"

Zack nodded and once again flicked the line, placing the fly in the center of the floating ring.

"Wow!"

She said the one breathless word with the same sense of wonder and excitement she had the night she had been surrounded by a roomful of armed men. "Show me?" she asked.

Zack felt an unexpected tightening in his chest as she looked up at him so trustingly.

"Please, Zack. Will you show me how to do that? I've read the book, so it's not like you have to start from the beginning. I mean, I know how it's supposed to be done, but I don't know how all those words *feel*, you know?"

"Yeah," he said. The tightening had spread from his chest to his throat, and Zack had to work to speak around it, had to work to hide an impossible moisture in his eyes. "Sure," he said, fumbling with the line for a moment before bending down to hand her the rod. "Like this," he told her, placing her little hands properly. "Now—"

He cleared his throat. "Now," he said, moving to stand behind her and placing his hands over hers, "you hold the line like this.... That's right. And this hand so.... That's right. And flick— That's right, Mickie."

Quickly, he stepped away from her. "Now you try."

The fly fell to the left of the ring, but Mickie was grinning as she reeled in the line. "Okay," she said, repositioning the line and the rod. "What did I do wrong?"

"Wrong? I didn't see anything wrong."

"I missed, Zack. Obviously I did something wrong. So, what do I do to correct it?"

And obviously this bright child didn't want any compliments or platitudes about how well she had done. Zack studied the problem for a moment. "Show me again," he said.

And again Mickie positioned the line and rod and her slender little body. Zack almost grinned when he saw the resolute expression on her tiny features, but he suspected she would resent anything resembling his laughing at her and quickly wiped the grin from his face. But while he was still looking at her expression, he noticed what he hadn't seen before. Her eyes squinted in determination, and one was squeezed tightly closed.

"Relax," he said. "Open both eyes and look at the ring."

"I suppose you don't want me biting my lip, either," she muttered.

Zack did laugh then, but he knew it was all right to do so. "Try it," he urged her.

The fly landed less than a foot from the ring.

"Again," he said.

And in it went.

And against his legs Mickie flung herself in celebration, catching him off-balance and off guard so that there was nothing for him to do but open his arms and squeeze her tight in response to her unbridled affection, dodging fishing rod and line, and fighting the tightness in his chest and throat and eyes that now threatened to overwhelm him.

"I guess," he said thickly, "that now the goldfish are in serious danger."

Mickie giggled. "I wouldn't hurt them," she said. "They're pets. But would you take me fishing, Zack?" She backed away from him to look up at him earnestly. "To a real river. Not now. I know we can't go anywhere now. But after the bad man is caught. Will you? Please?"

"Mickie—" *Oh, God, this hurt so bad.* Not that Barbara had told her child about the danger; that seemed almost inevitable. But that he couldn't promise her anything. Not that he would ever again see her after Barbara left him again. Not that he would have the strength to spend time with this child if her mother stayed.

"I know you're busy," Mickie said, her grin fading as she turned and reeled in her line.

"No, I—" Once again he found himself fighting to speak around the tightness in his throat. But—*damn it!*—he wanted to spend time with this child. And—*damn it!*—he never again wanted to see the bleak desolation that had blanked all expression and animation from her eyes. "I don't know what's going to happen, Mickie," he promised softly, "but if there is ever any way I can, I will take you fishing."

He knew by the way she looked back up at him that she had heard and believed the honesty in his voice. The twist of her lips almost made it to smile status. "Thank you," she said. "I'll be really good by then," she said. "Except you'll probably have to teach me how to reel in—" she glanced at the book, the pages of which were now fluttering in a light breeze "—I mean, *land* the fish. Unless you really don't mind my practicing on the goldfish."

He saw the gleam of mischief in her eyes. *My God,* he thought. *She's a handful.* Was there anything this child couldn't do? Yes, there was. And he'd better not let himself forget it. As bright as she was, Mickie couldn't understand the convoluted emotional maze that kept the three of them—her, Zack, and Barbara—trapped in this penthouse and yet separate from each other.

"Leave the goldfish alone, imp," he said lightly, giving her a mock cuff to her elfin chin. Only then did he look up to see Barbara standing in the shadows of the foliage, tears running unchecked down her cheeks as she watched the two of them together. Their eyes locked and he couldn't look away, even though he knew he should turn his attention to Mickie who didn't need to see her mother crying. "Now," he said to the child that should have been—*could* be—his, growing used to the tightening in his throat, "I want to see you land that fly in the ring again."

He watched as Barbara's hand flew to her mouth, as she stood there, immobile except for the slight rocking motion she made before she turned silently and hurried back to her room.

Zack stayed in his room the remainder of the afternoon, but the solitude he had sought evaded him. First the memories of a sylphlike child and a tawny-haired woman, her hazel eyes drenched by tears, haunted him. Then the sounds of Mickie and Dianne in the pool for Dianne's daily exercise, joined by Barbara's voice as she played with the girls while she worked Dianne through her therapist's program, intruded, almost driving him back downstairs to his office. Almost.

He resisted until the hour before dinner, the time when everyone should be dressing or otherwise occupied. Then, unable to fight his need to see Barbara, to hold her, to share with her, even silently, the emotions he had felt as she had watched him with her daughter, he went to her room.

The French doors stood open to capture any breeze, but the sheer curtains barely moved in the early evening air. Zack tapped once, quietly, but received no response, so he pushed aside the curtains and stepped inside.

He found Barbara curled on the chaise longue. With none of the laughter he had heard as she'd played with the girls earlier visible to animate her finely drawn features, he saw clearly the signs of the strain of the last few weeks. He also saw her complete lack of surprise as he walked into her room, her complete lack of welcome, or of rejection, only a deep, quiet resignation.

She sat up, but tucked her legs beneath her, managing to look both prim and alluring in the softly pleated voile skirt and blatantly romantic blouse. Mrs. Thompson had chosen well, with little more than a few words from him about Barbara's earlier taste in clothes and his preferences.

He glanced at the end of the chaise and, with a shrug, seated himself beside her. Since what he wanted to do was pull her into his arms, he clasped his hands together and rested his elbows on his knees, leaning forward, studying the nap of the carpet rather than looking at her.

When she remained silent, Zack drew a deep breath and squared his shoulders.

"I know I should be thinking of you, your fears, your pain," he told her, still not looking at her, "and please know that I am." He lifted his clasped hands and rested his chin on them. "But sometimes, like today, I feel so... so *damn* cheated."

"I know," Barbara said softly. "I know."

"Why couldn't you have let me know? Why couldn't you have trusted me enough to... to at least have let me help you, to have let me know her as she was growing up, to... to find some way out of this.... this morass we're caught in?"

"So you could have spent six more years in the hell you've been in since you learned about her?"

Zack didn't answer her; he couldn't answer her.

And Barbara didn't appear to expect an answer. "I prayed that she would look like you," she told him, her voice low, devoid of expression. "For months, even after she was born, I prayed that I would look at her and see your hair, or your eyes, or your coloring." She gave a soft, bitter laugh. "I don't recognize anything about her, except maybe the curl in her hair, because mine has that same unruly kink."

"But you won't have her tested."

"No. I lied. It's not only for Mickie's sake. *I* couldn't bear knowing that she is his child."

"And you wouldn't have an abortion."

"Zack, please!"

"Which means you knew there had to be a chance she was ours."

"It means only that I *wanted* her to be yours. I don't think any bookmaker gives odds simply on want."

"But you did."

He heard her muffled sob but still couldn't face her, couldn't watch as he said what had to be said. "You know we have to test her, Barbara. We can't begin to think of any kind of a life together with a question of that magnitude standing between us."

"Zack." He felt her hand on his cheek, a featherlight touch before she withdrew it. "More than the question of Mickie's birth stands between us. We can't begin to think of a life together at all."

Now he did turn. Her face was ashen, and she had caught her lower lip between her teeth as though biting back words he shouldn't hear. He reached for her, knowing he probably shouldn't, but also knowing there was no way he could continue to sit there without touching her. She didn't respond, but she didn't resist as he pulled her into the shelter of his arms.

"Can't we?" he asked. "Isn't that what both of us have been doing since I found you? Isn't that what our night together was really about?"

"No," she whispered, but he felt the shudder that racked her as though in response to her lie. He lifted her face and saw the tears that streamed steadily, quietly, from her lovely eyes.

So many tears, he thought. Hers. And the ones he had not let himself shed. How many more would there be? He clasped her against his chest, holding her cheek against his heart, knowing she could feel how unsteadily it beat—for her, for them. *No more,* he prayed. *Please save her—us—from the need for more tears.*

And then, working its way insidiously through his grief, his pain, his compassion for the woman he now held so protectively, came another, darker feeling.

Damn him! Hadn't Wilson's jealousy and hate caused enough pain in the past? *Why?* Why was he again putting all of them on the rack?

It wasn't anger that Zack felt. Anger was much too tame, too clean a word for the emotion that now battered him, leaving him with a knowledge he was afraid he had to accept but from which everything decent in him recoiled. Wilson would destroy them, all of them, for no sane reason. Unless Zack destroyed him first.

Ten

Meg was gone. In a flurry of last-minute changes. Without her laptop computer. Without her dictation unit. Without her file on her current project. In fact, if Barbara hadn't noticed the papers on Meg's dresser beside the envelope from that persistent alternate publisher and scooped the whole stack into a leather folio and tucked it into her garment bag, Meg wouldn't even have the notes for her speech.

But she did have Taylor Adams, looking gruff and stern and worried. And deadly competent. And Barbara knew she had no reason to worry about her friend.

She did, however, worry about her friend's daughter. Dianne had been unusually upset by her mother's departure. Even after the promise of a new tropical bird as a reward, the child had continued to shed silent tears until Taylor had practically dragged Meg from the apartment to catch their flight. And in a manner alien to her usual accepting attitude, Dianne had sulked the balance of the day and had even refused to participate in her regular exercises in the swimming pool.

Mickie had noticed. And had practically driven Barbara frantic with her efforts to cheer her friend, all of them requiring some sort of group effort.

The one good thing about the day was that Barbara had been so busy she hadn't had time to dwell on Zack's disturbing visit of the night before. But now the time for dinner approached and for the first time in hours, she was alone. All she really wanted to do as she waited in her room for the time to go in to dinner was to sink into a deep, dreamless sleep, but she knew that wouldn't happen. The long, sleepless hours of the night before had proven that to her.

Zack wanted her to stay.

Fool! she screamed silently. Fool, idiot, and incompetent that she was, she had let him know that she still loved him, had let him hope there was a chance she would stay.

And she couldn't.

Not as long as Wilson Truett lived and hated.

Not even if Zack was beginning to love her daughter.

She heard a quick tattoo of a knock on her bedroom door before it was thrust open and Mickie scampered in.

"Aren't you ready yet, Mom? Mrs. Thompson's got this really neat Italian thing for supper tonight, and it smells like it's just ready to eat, and I've got Dianne in the dining room already, and she's smiling for a change, and—"

"All right," Barbara said, laughing and holding her hands up in surrender. "Let's go. I'm ready."

But was she ready to face Zack again, to see but not answer the questions in his eyes, to want but not take the comfort of his arms, to love him but never, never tell him? She doubted that she would ever be.

There were just four of them for dinner, Barbara realized with dismay. No frowning Taylor or preoccupied Meg or even soft-spoken Jamie to distance her, literally and figuratively, from the man who was her husband. Only the children. Thank God for the children. Even if Dianne was sinking back into the sulks.

"Mother never leaves me," Dianne confided to Zack with just a hint of a tremor to her lip. "She always takes me and Barbara and Mickie, and while she's busy, we play or go shopping, and when she's not busy, we go to the museums and if there's anything really big and important, like Disneyland or Six Flags nearby, we all go to that together. So I don't know why—" She sniffed and lifted her chin with a bravado that had Barbara wondering if she might be destined to be the next generation's favorite actress. "I don't know why she had to go off with just *Taylor* this time."

Aha, Barbara thought. *That* was the underlying problem. Not being left behind, but being left behind while her mother went off with Taylor. She saw the glimmer in Zack's eyes that told her he, too, had recognized the problem, and she glanced at her daughter to see if Mickie had picked up on Dianne's jealousy as quickly as she had picked up on Meg and Taylor's interest in each other.

But Mickie was busy working her way through Mrs. Thompson's melt-in-your-mouth lasagna served with a crisp spinach salad and crusty homemade rolls, and seemed oblivious to anything but food. Mickie? Oblivious to her surroundings? Suspicious, Barbara looked again, but either Mickie had perfected her innocent-angel act or she really was interested only in the lasagna. Curious, Barbara thought. Very curious.

"Are you not enjoying your stay with us, Dianne?"

With a start, Barbara realized she had left Zack to deal with Dianne and turned back to them, determined to save him from Dianne's sulks or her list of *whys* that could be as bad as Mickie's.

"Of course I am, Mr. Gordon. I love my room and the pool and the games on the computer, and Jamie, and even that nasty old cat that Mickie hides in her room."

Barbara heard a muffled sound from her daughter and answered one of her earlier questions. Mickie was definitely not oblivious. But what was she up to? And why did Dianne's sulk now seem not quite so genuine as it had earlier in the day?

"You do believe by now that Tesla won't hurt your birds, don't you, Dianne?" Barbara asked.

"I guess."

"And that your mother will be home in three days?"

"Um."

Yes. The poor-pitiful-me routine was definitely beginning to sound like early histrionics.

"And that she wouldn't dare not bring you that cockatoo the conference committee located for her?"

Dianne looked up at her, forgetting her budding career in her enthusiasm. "It has a *twenty*-word vocabulary."

"So I've heard," Barbara said.

"But it's..." The young Sarah Bernhardt made a return appearance in the guise of a ten-year-old. "It's not enough to make me—to make me not miss my mother."

"Of course it isn't," Mickie said jovially, finally looking up from her lasagna. "That's why I think we need to do something tonight, you know, all together, to take Dianne's mind off Meg's abandoning her.'

"Mickie!"

"Well, temporarily abandoning her," Mickie amended. "I thought—" She grinned over at Zack in a blatant attempt to cajole him into doing what she wanted. "I thought maybe you could teach us to play poker."

Zack, watching her antics with some obvious but discreet amusement, had just taken a sip of his ice tea when Mickie made this pronouncement. He coughed, choking on his drink, and then carefully set his glass down. "Poker?" he asked. He glanced at Barbara. "Is that appropriate for... for girls their age?"

Barbara shrugged in answer to his question, grimaced, and turned to her daughter. "How much practice have you had?"

Mickie glanced at her plate, saw she had nothing remaining there to focus her attention on, and looked innocently across the room. "Well, I have played the computer game a few times."

"And?" Barbara insisted.

"And...and a couple of times with some people on one of the networks I've been able to get into with my new modem."

"And?"

"Aw, Mom." Once again Mickie looked at Zack, pleading and innocence written, with some exaggeration, on her features. "It's like the fishing, Zack," she said earnestly. "I know the rules, and I've even taught those to Dianne, but we don't really know how it's supposed to *feel*. So if you could just play with us, you know, a few games, so that we had more than just...just what comes out of books—"

Zack chuckled. "How often do you win, Mickie?"

Mickie hung her head. "All the time," she mumbled. "But that's when I'm playing the computer, and that's only a little kids' version of the game. I almost never win when I'm playing a real person."

"Except when that person is me," Dianne said, and then giggled when Mickie frowned at her. "Well, it's true."

"Barbara?" Zack asked.

And of course, now she knew what her daughter, with Dianne's help, was up to. Matchmaking. Getting her and Zack to spend time together, and with her. Artlessly pursuing her own innocent desires while inflicting havoc on the emotions of those she dragged along with her.

Barbara met Zack's troubled gaze across the table but hadn't a clue as to whether he was asking her permission to deny Mickie's plea or to commit them to an evening together. And she hadn't a clue as to what he ought to do. "It's...it's up to you."

And in the time it took for her to voice her answer, Barbara saw realization dawn in Zack's eyes. *He knew.* He knew Mickie was plotting. And before he opened his mouth, Barbara knew what his answer would be.

"I think..." he said, raising his glass in a salute to Mickie—obviously he saw no need to hide his recognition of her scheming. "I think that the four of us spending the evening together—at poker—might prove to be interesting."

"Interesting" didn't begin to describe the evening. Sometime after the move from the dining room to a table in Zack's cozy study, Barbara discovered an even greater acting ability than she had ever suspected she had. She found she was able to speak, to deal competently with the cards when necessary, to laugh, even to watch the two people she loved most in the world struggling to find their way with each other without succumbing to the tears and despair she felt struggling to break free.

"This is only a way of keeping score," Zack told the girls as he distributed a generous supply of poker chips to each of them. "You can play without betting, and that's what we'd do if I thought this was teaching you that the abuse of gambling isn't dangerous, but this game is more fun when there's something at stake."

But not when everything is at stake! Barbara thought before fiercely reminding herself that the cat-and-mouse game Wilson Truett played with them was no game at all.

Zack led the girls through a few different versions of poker to determine which they preferred, as well as their skill levels, before passing the deck to Dianne to deal, coaching them in how to ante, call and raise, giving them suggestions on how to decide what to discard, then guiding each of them through the responsibilities as dealer. Barbara watched Dianne win, watched Mickie win, even noted that her own pile of chips managed to stay about the same size, before the deck returned still another time to Zack, and the pile of plastic betting chips in the center of the table began to grow as the betting passed around the table once, then twice, then started a third time.

Barbara folded her cards and opted out of the game. After a few anguished frowns, Dianne also folded, leaving Zack and Mickie the only competitors in what now appeared to be a deadly serious round of what was supposed to have been light entertainment.

Finally Mickie sighed and threw down her cards. "You win," she said. "But I don't know how you could. I had a really great hand and—"

"Then why didn't you continue to bet? Why did you concede?"

"Because you had to have something so much better than I did or you wouldn't have kept on betting. What was it, Zack? A royal flush? It couldn't have been four aces, cause I had two of them. Show me."

"You know I don't have to, don't you?"

"You don't?"

Zack shook his head. "Not unless you call the bet."

"But that means I'd have to risk losing even more. That's not fair."

"Life's not always fair, pumpkin."

Barbara heard the pain creep back into Zack's voice. "He may not have a winning hand, Mickie," she said, trying to remind him that this was, after all, just a game.

"What? Then why would he bet all those chips? And if he doesn't have anything, don't I win?"

Zack grinned as he reached forward and dropped his cards faceup on the table.

"A pair of twos," Mickie said, incredulous. "A lousy pair of twos and I let you win?"

"It's called bluffing, and it's one of the most important things to learn about this game. But you didn't *let* me win. I knew I probably didn't have a winning hand, but I did have a pretty good idea of how you play."

"I still don't think it's fair," Mickie mumbled as she pushed the poker chips across the table to Zack. Half an hour later, though, she won a proud smile from Zack and the round with no more than a queen by using the same tactics. And Dianne quickly grasped the idea, too, calling Mickie's bluff a few hands later and reclaiming a sizable stack of chips.

Even though Mickie remained enthusiastic, by that time Dianne was yawning and Zack was beginning to show some signs of the strain Barbara felt. Quietly Barbara gathered the cards and shuffled them into a neat stack. "I believe it's bedtime," she said.

"Aw, Mom—" Mickie began, but a huge yawn from Dianne stopped her in midprotest.

"Aw, Mickie," Barbara echoed. "Come on," she said, rising from the table and walking to stand between Mickie and Dianne, bending down to fold both girls into a double hug. "Let's get the two of you tucked in. You can plot and plan some more tomorrow."

She watched Mickie's eyes widen as she realized she had been caught by her mother in a manipulation and apparently decided withdrawal was wise. But she didn't go without one last tug on Barbara's heart. Slipping from her chair, Mickie hurried over to Zack and gave him a quick, fierce hug. "Thank you," she said. "I had the best time, ever." Then she grabbed Dianne's hand and hurried her out of the room, leaving Barbara alone with Zack.

Zack continued to sit at the table, very quiet, very still, as he stared at the doorway through which the girls had run.

"Yes," Barbara told him. "Thank you. I know how hard this must have been for you to do, and I—"

"Don't you have to see that the girls get to bed?" Zack asked.

"Yes. Yes, I do."

"Then why don't you do that? But come back." He looked at her then, and she saw all too clearly just *how* hard the evening had been for him. "We'll have a...a drink. I think we both need one."

She found him standing near the table in the garden after she had finally gotten the girls tucked in. But instead of the drink he had suggested, he had brought cups and a carafe of coffee from the kitchen.

"I thought we probably were in enough of a muddle without adding the effects of alcohol," he said as he handed her a cup. "Are you all right?"

Barbara noticed that her hands were trembling as she took the cup, a trembling that only increased as her fingers brushed against Zack's. But if Zack noticed, he said nothing, and she retreated quickly to the security of a chair beneath her and a table between her and the temptation of walking into Zack's embrace and telling him that was where she wanted to stay.

"I've been thinking," he told her. "About Mickie. And about what you said last night. About there not being a life together for the two of us."

"Don't. Please, don't."

"Why not, Barbara? Because if I confront you with what I want, if I force you to discuss your reasons why you can't stay, you might discover that you *want* to stay? You might discover enough trust in me to begin to believe that I can keep you safe, that I can provide a home for you and—and for Mickie? My God, you have to know I wouldn't do anything to hurt your child!"

"I know you wouldn't willingly to anything to hurt anyone, Zack. Except maybe yourself if I were—if *we* were to stay with you. But—"

God! this was hard. Harder than anything she had already faced. Because as Zack did force her to discuss her reasons for leaving—those that she could admit to him—she *did* find them lacking; she *did* find herself trusting him to keep her safe, and she wanted more than ever the home he could provide for her.

But what *she* wanted or needed couldn't count, even if Wilson was captured. And if he wasn't... If he wasn't, fear of what he could do in the future assured her that there could be no life for her with Zack.

Barbara set her cup on the table and stood, thinking that standing might make her feel less vulnerable. It didn't, but holding herself very erect, pretending that it did, she walked to Zack's side.

She felt pain and frustration, even rage, emanating from him, and recognized all of those emotions, because she felt them, too. Once she had thought they had everything good that life had to offer. Now they had nothing, except memories that she had to keep locked securely away, because remembering their time together before Wilson had torn them apart made it almost impossible for her to do what must be done.

But, oh, what she wouldn't give for just a few more clean, untainted memories to take with her, to hold to herself in the wasteland where her heart would have to dwell when she again left Zack.

"I can't promise you forever," she heard herself saying, unable to stop from moving closer to him, unable to stop words that should never be said. "But I can promise you these three days."

Zack turned, looking down at her, his eyes glittering in the dim light surrounding the pool.

"Until Meg returns," she continued softly. "Just until Meg returns."

Barbara found Zack's room as familiar as an old friend when they entered through the French doors. The little art-nouveau lamp cast a welcoming, comforting glow across the sedately patterned Oriental rug, the gleaming walnut of the wardrobe, and a corner of king-size bed, and the slight summer breeze whispered lazily through the sheer curtains covering the doorway. But that was the only comfort she felt as Zack closed the doors and drew the draperies to cover them.

What she was doing was wrong! Zack believed that he could change her mind, that he could convince her to stay. She knew that as certainly as she knew that she could never stay, as certainly as she knew she couldn't stop herself from taking this time with him.

"I love you, Barbara," he said as he cupped her face with his hands.

And I love you.

The silence screamed her unspoken words, hurtling them through her mind, through her heart. If Zack listened with *his* heart, he would hear them, too, and that was something else that could never—*should* never—happen.

She lifted her fingers to his mouth, to silence him, but found herself tracing his lips with her fingertips, found herself stepping closer to him, into his embrace as she had wanted to do all evening, felt the deep shudder that shook Zack's powerful frame as he moved his hands from her cheeks to her back and enveloped her with his warmth, with his strength, with his love.

She felt her breath leaving her as she stretched upward to meet him, as Zack lowered his head, as his mouth sought hers.

"We ought to talk," he whispered against her mouth. "I know that, know we need to resolve so many things and that if I kiss you, if I touch you, talk is the last thing we will do. But, Barbara, I need this, too—I need *you*—more than I can tell you, more than any words can ever convey."

He didn't need words to tell her. God help her, she *knew*, because she needed him every bit as much as he needed her. And unlike Zack, she knew that *talk* was the last thing they *should* do.

Trailing her hand to the back of Zack's head, Barbara tugged slightly, until there was no room between them for words, no room between them for anything but assauaging the ache in her heart by appeasing that other physical ache that Zack knew so well how to ignite.

She heard him groan and knew the moment he surrendered his need for her words to his need for her passion. That need she could answer, did answer, as she let her hands and lips and body touch him in ways he had long ago taught her to please him, and she felt his hands and lips and body touching her in ways he had long ago learned to please her.

This was not the gentle, hesitant lover she had met again after years of separation; this was the Zachary Gordon of her memory: strong, confident, sometimes impatient in his passion but always careful to make sure he took her with him in his search for fulfillment.

She felt the sheets, crisp and cool against her flesh as later he lowered her to the bed, and wondered, for a moment, how they had managed to divest themselves of their clothes, but then Zack resumed his needy campaign to drive her stark, raving mad with her own needs.

She felt him hesitate, felt him move away from her, heard the drawer of the bedside table slide open, and had to fight to keep herself from crying out for him to forget protection, to do as he had once said he wanted—to make her pregnant and force her to stay with him forever. But she did remain silent as she heard the package rip open, and then, this time, she remained passive until he once again took her in his arms and with his touch erased all thought of protest or protection.

"I love you, Barbara," Zack said again as at last he united them.

For a moment, his voice grated with something akin to desperation.

For a moment, his hands gripped her tightly, harshly.

For a moment, his mouth plundered hers, taking rather than seeking.

And for a moment, Barbara was thrown back to a memory of other hands, other words, another time.

No! She wouldn't—couldn't—let those memories intrude on her time with Zack. So much between them had already been touched with the ugliness of Wilson's hate. This was to have been—*would be*—an untainted moment she carried forever in her heart.

And I love you, my darling, she told Zack silently as she moved against him, with him, striving only to give him pleasure and in so doing finding her own.

Zack lay awake in the middle of the night, roused by dreams and by the slight pressure of Barbara's body curved so trustingly against him.

Three days, she had promised him. So much less than he wanted from her. So much more than the *now* that was all she had been able to promise only days before.

Thank God, you were not the one to have to kill someone. The words of Barbara's farewell letter to him mocked him. He'd wanted to then. And when he saw the fear in Barbara's eyes or heard it in her voice, he wanted to now. How much could a man take before he broke? Before he violated every tenet he held sacred? Before he killed to protect what was more precious to him than his own life?

He hadn't protected Barbara in the past, and she had left him. Now she promised to leave him again, and he knew the reason: fear—fear that he would not protect her in the future.

He would never let Wilson's twisted hate touch Barbara again, but how could he make her see that? What would it take to convince her that he could keep her and Mickie safe? Would anything less than killing his stepbrother be enough?

Zack felt a chill rack his body with that thought.

As though aware of the deep and murky paths Zack's thoughts had taken, Barbara moaned in her sleep and turned, snuggling closer to him.

Three days, Zack thought as he felt his body's immediate response to her innocent movements. Three days, and one was almost gone.

Slowly, subtly, he shifted and turned until he faced her. The dim light from the lamp caught in the waves of her luxurious hair before dancing over her slender, graceful body. She was his. She had promised him before God and man and the State of Georgia that she would always be his. But even if she had never made that promise, Zack knew he could never let her go . . . could never lose her again.

Softly, with a patience he was far from feeling, he lifted his hand and lightly traced the upper curve of her breast, teasing her with gentle motions until he saw her eyes open, saw her mouth curve in a smile that was all feminine lure, and felt her lean into his touch and lift her hand to begin a gentle exploration of her own.

Eleven

Three days. An eternity, and yet gone in an instant. Ecstasy, yet agony.

And in spite of the charade she and Zack each maintained, that of being, for this short moment out of time, a couple again, with the right to love, the right to plan, the right to laugh, Barbara never quite forgot it *was* a charade, never quite forgot the threat of Wilson Truett looming in the future, never quite forgot that Zack wasn't and never could be as at ease with her daughter as he pretended to be. Except...except at night, in Zack's arms, she almost let herself believe they could have a future together.

Until their three days were used up, their nights only a memory. Until the day when Meg was to return, the day that marked the end of the time that Barbara had given them.

Zack woke her that last morning by taking her in his arms and loving her with such tenderness that later she had no strength to hold back the tears she had fought for so long.

"It doesn't have to be over," Zack told her, holding her possessively, protectively, against himself while he traced the path of her tears with one tentative hand. "You were the one who set the limits, you can change them."

"No. I can't."

"Why?" Wrapping both arms around her, pulling her even more tightly into his embrace, Zack shuddered and fought for control. "Why?" he asked again, his voice calmer now but far from calm. "Why should Meg's return have anything to do with our being together?"

"Meg's and Taylor's," Barbara said.

"Is that supposed to make any sense?"

Barbara almost told him that it made perfect sense; that she had stolen three days for herself and now that time was up; that she would never be able to convince him or anyone else she didn't love him when she left again if she didn't end this interlude now. But of course she couldn't tell him that. "No," she said instead. "I suppose not.

"Please, Zack," she said, knowing it was once again time to start living the lie. "Don't ask more of me than I have to give."

She felt him tense, felt him gathering his words and arguments for another onslaught, but instead he released her and rolled away.

Already she missed his warmth and his touch. She wanted to follow him, to tell him that she would stay with him forever if he would only hold her safe, if he would only... But she couldn't do that, either.

"I suppose we'd better get up," he said dully. "If we're not at the breakfast table, Mickie might come looking for you."

You wouldn't want her to find you with me.

Barbara heard those words as clearly as though Zack had said them, and knew that he, too, had other things he wouldn't say, couldn't say.

"Yes," she told him, and her voice sounded as dull to her ears as his had. "I suppose we must."

Breakfast was a miserable, quiet meal. The girls had apparently picked up on the emotions of the adults, and nothing Barbara said or did lightened the mood. When Zack finally pushed back from the table and excused himself, she almost sighed with relief at finally being able to escape to the privacy of her room.

But that wasn't to happen.

"Will you walk with me to the elevator?" Zack asked, but she heard more command than invitation in his voice.

"Of course," she said quietly, folding her napkin and placing it carefully beside her plate, hiding the tremor in her hands as she, too, rose.

Just before they reached the foyer, Zack turned and captured her face in his hands.

"This isn't over yet," he said harshly as he bent and took her mouth in a kiss that shouted of his possession.

No, it would never be over, she thought as she surrendered willingly, one last time, to her love for him. Not in her lifetime. And, God, it was getting harder and harder for her to remember why it must be.

Noises intruded. Zack pulled away, reluctantly, before Barbara identified the sounds: voices, Jamie's and Mr. Tewksbury's, the sound of the elevator doors closing.

"It's not over," Zack whispered, still holding her arm as he turned and led her into the foyer.

"Morning, boss," Jamie said pleasantly, still holding a stack of envelopes, which he handed to Barbara. "I got drafted into bringing Meg's mail," he told her. "Oh," he added as he keyed in the code to open the elevator doors and dropped an innocent verbal bomb. "There's one for you. Maybe a card from Meg?"

Zack stopped and turned, holding the door open while Barbara sorted quickly through the envelopes. Mail for her? No one ever wrote to her, and from the tension she felt emanating from Zack, he knew that as well as she did.

It was an oddly shaped envelope, greeting card size, and her name and Zack's address were printed on a computer label. The postmark was smeared and illegible. She ripped the envelope open and drew out the card. The larger card shops now carried computer personalization equipment; Barbara didn't know if this had come from one of those shops, or if the message had been added later, in the privacy of an office. The card was simple: the cover carried a photograph of a scenic street scene in downtown Atlanta, a scene well remembered by Barbara. The message was simple, too, just two words: *Missing you.*

"*Zack!*"

She could no more have stopped from crying out his name than she could have stopped the panic that first stopped her heart, then started it in a mad race.

Instantly he was beside her, taking the card from her, glancing at it before thrusting it at Jamie. "Get this to our contact at the FBI."

She heard Jamie's answer, but couldn't have said later what it was. "I'm all right," she heard herself saying. "Really, I'm all right." But she wasn't; she knew that, she just didn't know how to release her grip on Zack's arms, how to stop her voice and her hands from trembling, how to bend down and pick up the mail that lay scattered at her feet. "Why now?" she asked him. "Why now?"

"Mom?"

Mickie's voice sobered her. She glanced up at Zack, warning him to silence.

"Mom, is something wrong?"

"No, Mickie," she heard Zack say. *Never lie to your child.* Instructions from every book on childhood development mocked her. *Except when the truth is unbearable.* Silently she amended each of those manuals. *Except when you can't face the truth yourself.* "Your mother just . . . She—"

"She slipped," Barbara heard Jamie say, "and dropped the mail."

"Oh. Well, good—I mean, that the mail is here, not that you slipped. Is my. . . Is there . . . ? Did I—?"

Barbara saw Jamie glance at Zack and shrug. "You mean, did you get three big boxes addressed to you in care of Zack's office?"

"What?"

Zack's question mingled with hers.

"Sorry, Zack. We were holding them downstairs until we could check them out, but it looks as though Mickie has vouched for them as well as spilling what appears to have been some very secret beans.''

"Three boxes?'' Barbara found her voice. "Mickie, what on earth have you done now?''

"I just... Well, I—I ordered them off the bulletin boards... you know, on the computer. I didn't expect *three* boxes. But don't worry, I can return everything—''

"And how were you going to pay for them?'' Barbara heard her voice rising, felt her temper soaring as her mind latched onto something, anything, that she could confront. She felt Zack's hands tighten on her arms as he gave a small warning shake of his head.

"I'll take care of this,'' he told her softly. "Mickie, Jamie is going to be late for your lessons this morning. I think you and Dianne had better find something quiet to do until he can get back to you.''

"You bet.'' Recognizing an escape when she saw it, Mickie made a hasty retreat.

"I'm sorry,'' Barbara said. "I'm so sorry. I don't know why I fell apart like that. I—''

"Jamie, go on downstairs. I'll be there later, but first I'll take Barbara to her room.''

"No,'' she said. The last thing she wanted now was to go to her room, to be alone with her thoughts. Or alone with Zack. "Really. I'm—I'll be all right. Please, Zack.'' She glanced around, seeing the concerned expressions on Jamie's face, on Mr. Tewksbury's face. On Zack's face. In search of something less troubling, she looked down at the mail at her feet.

"Please,'' she said again. "Go do what you have to do.''

What Zack had to do was try to make some sense out of a situation that made no sense. What he had to do was wait for Taylor to return. What he had to do was forcibly restrain himself from going upstairs, taking Barbara in his arms and holding her there until all threat to her had been demolished.

Taylor and Meg arrived just before noon. Zack had left word with the door guard so he had been notified in time to meet them as they stepped off the elevator.

Meg looked as distraught as Barbara had earlier. Taylor didn't look much better, but when he saw Zack, he turned to Meg. "Go on upstairs," he told her, summoning the penthouse elevator for her. "I'll bring your things up later."

"What's wrong?" he asked Zack the moment the elevator doors closed.

"That's my question," Zack said as they walked into his office and closed the door.

Taylor shook his head. "She forgot the bird."

"What?"

"Meg's been distracted since halfway through the conference. I thought she was worried about being separated from her daughter, but then she forgot to buy the damn bird for Dianne. What's happened here?"

"A card," Zack told him. "Addressed to Barbara."

"From Truett?"

"Unsigned. 'Missing you,' it said. No demand. No explanation. Damn it!" Zack slammed his fist against his desk. "What does he want? And what is he waiting for?"

Taylor had no answer, but as the two men faced each other in silence, the telephone rang.

"Adams," Taylor said, picking up the receiver. "Right. Send it up."

He replaced the receiver and straightened away from the desk. "Another delivery," he said, grim-faced.

I trust Mr. Adams enjoyed his small vacation, read the dot-matrix printed note wrapped around the videotape, *and that your lovely wife received her card.*

"Damn!" Zack's hand clenched on the note Taylor handed him. "Does he know everything that goes on here? And if so, how?"

Taylor slammed the tape into the player. "I don't know. But maybe he's getting tired of waiting, too."

Zack leaned back against his desk, waiting for the next installment in torture. But what he saw held him frozen in shock for several seconds before he was able to grab the remote and stop the tape.

"Zack?"

The television was dark but still the pictures unfolded in his mind. Images of Barbara, not knowing what was to come but facing it with a bravado that had the ability now, as it had seven years ago, to bring him to tears.

"Zack? What is it?"

He saw his hand holding the remote, saw the familiar furnishings of his office surrounding him, even heard the concern in Taylor's voice, but all of that was unreal. What was real was on that tape. What was real was the truth that nothing he could say or do would ever erase that reality from his life or from Barbara's.

"Zack? Why did you turn off the tape?"

"It's the first tape he sent me," Zack said, hearing a thickness in his voice, feeling an unaccustomed slowness in his motions as he turned to face Taylor. "I know everything that's on it. I've seen everything that's on it a thousand times, in my dreams, in my memories. I don't have to—I *will not* watch it again."

"That bastard."

"Possibly," Zack said, feeling curiously detached from the room and from the conversation. "Although his mother really was a lovely woman."

"You have to watch it."

Zack looked over at Taylor. "Never again," he swore.

"Don't you understand? If you don't, we'll never know if his warped mind decided this was an appropriate way to send you a message."

"Or perhaps just an appropriate way to send me to hell?"

"There is that possibility," Taylor said, "but if you don't watch it, we'll never know. Do you . . . do you want me to watch it for you?"

Zack closed his eyes, remembering too well what Taylor would see and knowing he could never let that happen.

"No." He sighed and tried to relax, but could not release his death grip on the remote. "Go to the outer office," he said, acknowledging that he knew what must be done. "This won't take long."

"Zack, I—"

Zack straightened away from the desk and from the sympathy he heard in the other man's voice. "Just go, Taylor. I'll let you know if there's a message."

As Taylor suspected, Truett had included a message, but he had insured that Zack would have to watch every agonizing frame of the tape before receiving it.

Feeling battered himself, Zack rewound the tape and walked carefully to his office door. He opened it and wordlessly summoned Taylor into the office and closed the door.

"We'll have instructions tomorrow," he told Taylor. "Make whatever preparations you think necessary. And Taylor," he said, remembering the tape, remembering a vow he had made to himself only three nights before, a vow that he now feared could be kept in only one way. "Get me a gun."

What had happened to Meg? Barbara watched her friend pace restlessly around her room. The scene with Dianne had been heartbreaking, with Dianne and eventually Meg both tearful. Dianne was too young to understand the fearful pressures on the adults; she knew only that her mother, for the first time ever, had broken a promise to her.

"This trip was supposed to have been good for you," Barbara said as Meg paused by the window, looking vacantly into the bright afternoon light. "What happened?"

"What happened?" Meg reached up and pulled the pins from her hair, letting it spill over her shoulders, and tossed the pins at the top of her dresser. "What happened is that I made love to a man I don't know. I blew a speech in front of some of the most respected people in my field. And I forgot a promise to my daughter. Not bad work for three days, was it?"

"Oh, Meg," Barbara said, zeroing in on what she suspected Meg least wanted to talk about—Barbara had read the speech and knew it couldn't have been that much of a failure, and Dianne would forgive her mother anything, after she got over the initial hurt. "You and Taylor?"

"I'm not happy about this, Barbara. I thought I had more—more personal integrity than to throw myself down in front of the first Clint Eastwood type that . . . that—"

"That had the good sense to see what a wonderful woman you are?"

"Hmpff!"

Barbara grinned when Meg cast an anguished glance at her and then stared at the floor. It was amazing how many different expressions that sound could convey.

"And since I'm pretty sure you've been celibate most if not all of the last seven years—ever since Dianne's father couldn't face the responsibility of raising her and left you to do it alone—I hardly think that succumbing to the obvious attraction you and Taylor have felt for each other casts you in the roll of fallen woman.

"Meg," she added when her friend continued to look steadfastly at the floor, "don't you know that your integrity can't be harmed because you care for someone? You're solid gold, my friend, and *nothing* can change that."

Meg looked up at her, then, her eyes washed with tears, her face crumpling. "I'm sorry," she said, and dashed angrily at her tears. "Please. I have to be alone for a while."

"Sure," Barbara told her, crossing to the door. "I'm going to see about the girls now, but I'll be just down the hall if you need to talk."

"Barbara, I . . ."

Barbara stopped on her way out the door and turned. "Yes, Meg?"

"I'm sorry," Meg whispered. "I—I . . . Thank you."

Zack came to her room that night. Not knocking, not asking permission, he opened the hall door and came in, then locked the door behind him. He walked to the side of the bed where Barbara had lain for hours, her mind spinning too madly to allow her to sleep, lifted the sheet, and slid into bed beside her. She stiffened only slightly, her mind telling her to protest, while her heart and body demanded that she welcome him.

But she felt no passion in Zack when he gathered her against him, just a quiet desperation.

He knew something. But he wasn't going to tell her. And for the moment, that was all right. For the moment, she didn't have to face any more horrors, any more fears. For the moment, all she needed to do, all she wanted to do, was hold and comfort the man she loved in the same way he now held and comforted her.

The message didn't come until almost noon. On a video-tape. How else? Zack wondered. But this tape contained nothing more than the message, as though Wilson were running out of time or patience, or perhaps just out of filmed footage. A meeting place. A time. A warning to come alone.

Zack wanted to go upstairs and— And what? Say good-bye? Or just hold Barbara. He hadn't seen her this morning; she had awakened before him, and he had heard the muffled sounds of her crying in her bathroom. He'd wanted to go to her then, but knew that if he had never come into her life, she would have had no reason to be hiding her tears in a bathroom. He wanted to go to her now, but felt, some-how, that only after he had confronted Wilson, had made sure that he would never again be a danger to anyone, would he have the right to touch her.

He rewound the tape and called Taylor into his office, waited while Taylor watched the message, then made the necessary calls, waited until Taylor produced the small, deadly snub-noised .357 revolver.

"Are you sure about this?" Taylor asked.

Zack tucked the revolver in position at the small of his back and shrugged into his suit coat. Was he? Probably not. But until he actually confronted Wilson, he had no way of knowing. "I'm sure. Are we ready?"

"As ready as we're ever going to be," Taylor told him.

"Then let's get this over with."

* * *

Barbara muttered a soft oath as once again the papers that she was trying to study blurred before her eyes. She pushed back from her desk and restlessly paced around her room. She had missed breakfast and, coward that she was, she had opted to hide out in her room during lunch rather than risk facing Zack across the table. Now Barbara realized that she was hungry. She chuckled. How amazing that something as mundane as a missed meal was finally able to drag her thoughts away from Zachary Gordon and what he knew but wasn't telling her.

She glanced at her watch, frowning at the time. She could have sworn several hours had passed since Mrs. Thompson had tried to entice her into coming to lunch instead of barely one. Shrugging at the vagaries of the human mind that made time seem to speed up or slow down, she left her room on a mission to raid another woman's kitchen.

She looked in on the girls as she passed their rooms, finding them happily ensconced in front of the computer in Mickie's room, without Jamie, which gave her cause for another frown, but they were oblivious to anything other than whatever game they were playing, and she didn't disturb them.

The penthouse seemed strangely quiet and lifeless as Barbara crossed through the living room, avoiding the foyer, cut through the breakfast room and started through the service hall toward the kitchen. She shook her head at the foolish thought that she was the only adult left in the apartment. All she had to do to disprove that was backtrack to the foyer and speak to Mr. Tewksbury, or search out Mrs. Thompson's quarters and disturb her while she was watching the soap opera Barbara had overheard her admitting to Meg that she was addicted to.

And besides, there was someone ahead of her in the hall.

Someone who was slipping furtively into the hallway from the kitchen.

Someone whose careful steps and motions screamed of stealth and secrecy.

Someone who was poking tentatively at the keypad of the electronic door lock.

Barbara came to an abrupt stop and studied the person who stood only a few steps away but was unaware of her presence.

"Meg?"

Meg whirled around and then smiled sheepishly. "I thought you were in your room." She had dressed in one of her "to the mall" outfits instead of the more casual outfits she wore at meals or the ratty sweats or jeans she usually wore when she worked, had pinned her hair up into a neat coil, and had applied makeup, but she still looked as though she were a wire stretched almost to the breaking point.

"Obviously, I'm not," Barbara said. "You're going somewhere?"

"What? Oh. Oh, well, yes, I am. I guess I should have told you."

"With Taylor?"

"Not exactly—I mean, no." Meg straightened her shoulders and looked directly at Barbara. "Not with Taylor. I have—I have to get out for a while. I have some things I need to think through, away from here, and I have...I have to get Dianne something to make up for forgetting that blasted cockatoo."

"Did you check this out with Taylor?"

"No. I didn't think it was necessary."

Barbara walked closer to her friend and studied her carefully.

"I know I told you we're not in prison, Meg—we aren't. But I'm not sure it's safe for you to go out alone."

"I'll be safe. Nobody has to worry about that." Barbara had less than a second to wonder about the bitterness she heard in Meg's voice. "I'm sorry about that scene yesterday, Barbara."

"There's nothing to be sorry about." Close enough now, Barbara reached out and touched Meg's arm. "What's wrong, Meg?"

"Nothing!" Meg drew in a deep breath. "Nothing. I just have to get out of here. Please understand, my sanity depends on it."

Should she tell her? Could she not tell her? "I think Zack and Taylor have heard something," Barbara said, knowing she had no choice. "I really wish you'd discuss this with one of them. Maybe . . . maybe Taylor could go with you."

"I can't." Meg leaned against the wall, away from Barbara's touch. "An hour, maybe two. That's all I need. Please, Barbara, I have to have this."

"You know the code? Taylor told you?"

Meg shook her head. "I *watched*. It's a three-digit code. All I had to do was look when we went downstairs, and when he sent me upstairs, I saw that it's the same as the one up here, only reversed. I suspected this door was probably keyed the same. I just checked. It is.

"So will you distract Dianne if she decides that she needs me and no one else until I get back?"

"Meg, I'm not sure about this."

"Trust me," Meg said, her voice breaking. "Just once more, please trust me."

"Of course," Barbara told her. "Always. It's just some other people in this world I don't trust, Meg. I don't want you hurt because of me."

"Zack and Taylor will be all right," Meg said. Quickly she keyed in and explained the simple code and opened the service door. "You and the girls will be safe, here, until they get back." She turned and gave Barbara a quick, unexpected hug. "You know that I've come to think of you as more than a friend. You're the sister I never had, and I would never, *never* intentionally hurt you."

Before Barbara could begin to think of an answer, Meg was gone, feet skipping rapidly down the stairs, and the heavy door closed, silencing the protest already forming on Barbara's lips.

Twelve

An hour, maybe two. That's all I need. That's all I need...

An hour had passed and still Meg's words echoed through Barbara's mind as she tried to convince herself her friend would be safe outside the compound. After all, she'd gone to the conference... *and had come back with her emotions stretched tighter than a drum.* Was her involvement with Taylor the sole cause of that?

Or had... Oh, God, had something else happened while Meg had been away?

Zack and Taylor will be all right. You and the girls will be safe here until they get back.

Until they get back? From where? And how had Meg known? Taylor Adams would never have revealed secrets Zack didn't want known. Not even to Meg.

Not even to Meg, who had dressed and applied makeup and had fixed her hair to go out—not a spur-of-the-moment decision because her thoughts and emotions were in turmoil, but a conscious, plotted action that took advantage of Mrs. Thompson's habits, the girls' well-known involve-

ment with their computer games, and Barbara's hermit act,
to ensure Meg could get away without being stopped.

Without telling anyone?

Would Meg have left without saying anything to anyone
if Barbara hadn't surprised her in the hallway? The Meg that
Barbara had shared a major part of her life with wouldn't
have. But maybe the one she had seen since Zack had
brought them here would.

Without stopping to argue herself out of invading her
friend's privacy, Barbara hurried to Meg's room. The room
was in shambles, with files and papers scattered across the
desk and Meg's working clothes dropped on the foot of the
bed along with other discarded clothing. But what stopped
Barbara in her tracks was the sight of the small fireproof
lockbox sitting open on the bed.

Barbara had both hated and needed the presence of Meg's
revolver in the house over the years, but both women had
been afraid of their small children finding it so it had been
kept locked in the box with Meg's car titles and insurance
policies, only taken out for periodic cleaning and trips to the
target range.

Had Meg taken the gun with her? Or had she left it at the
house? Because it wasn't in the lockbox. What was in the
lockbox, right on top, was a copy of the power of attorney
Meg had long before had prepared, giving Barbara the right
to care for Dianne in case of an emergency and see that she
got any necessary medical care, and a bundle of letters from
various publishers, none of them the one Meg wrote for
regularly. One letter had slid halfway from its envelope.
Barbara picked it up, recognizing the envelope with the for-
warding address as the one that had arrived since Zack had
brought them here, and unfolded the strange letterhead
stationery.

*It would be a shame for something to happen to Dianne
now that she's nearly well. Call me,* was scrawled in a heavy
black script. The words looked as ominous as their message, not professional at all. Her heart beating heavily,
Barbara reached for another. *Call me.* And another. *Call
me.* And another... going back—Barbara scrambled

through the envelopes, reading postmarks—going back years. *Call me.* But who or what or where?

"Oh, Meg," she whispered. "What have you done?"

Zack should be told she was gone and, as traitorous as it seemed to Meg, about the envelopes. But surely...oh, please, there had to be an explanation other than the one that screamed through Barbara's heart. And Taylor—maybe Taylor would have some idea where she had gone...and why. *If* they *were here.*

She backed away from the incriminating lockbox, turned and left the room. What she wanted to do was run, blindly, anywhere away from the menace that had shadowed everything in her life for so long. But she forced herself to give the appearance of calm as she approached the foyer.

Mr. Tewksbury looked up at her arrival and then stood.

"I need to go downstairs," she said, amazed at how calm she sounded.

He nodded. "Of course, Mrs. Gordon." Without so much as a question he walked to the elevator and keyed in the code. "You'll find everyone in the security offices."

A man she recognized from evening duty on the security desk in the foyer upstairs was hurrying toward her when the elevator doors opened onto the floor below. He waited only until she had stepped from the car. "This way, please," he said before turning back in the direction from which he had come.

He didn't seem to expect an answer as Barbara followed him across Zack's reception area, through double doors and into a spacious area filled with monitors and men.

"Are Zack and Taylor here?" she asked.

"No, they're not back yet," he told her, leading her through a cubicle divider at the end of the room into an area slightly less chaotic. Jamie stood in front of a large map. He wore a headset with a minuscule earphone and one of those tiny microphones that had somehow managed to take over the world in the time since she had dropped out. He looked up, for once not smiling, and pushed the mouthpiece to one side.

"I often wondered about your other job," Barbara told him, hesitant now to betray Meg, even though...even though the evidence seemed to indicate that *Meg* might have been the one doing the betraying.

"Is something wrong?" he asked, and even his voice sounded different: all business now.

Barbara nodded. "Meg's gone out." She realized she still held the bundle of letters. "I think she's in...in some serious trouble."

There was nothing else to do; she handed the letters to Jamie. He frowned as he scanned through them, but said nothing about their contents. "Do you know how long she's been gone?"

"About an hour," Barbara told him. "She said...she said she just needed an hour, maybe two, to think some things through."

He looked at the man who had met her at the elevator. "Johnson, I want you to go looking for Mrs. Riley. Take a car. Check out the neighborhood side streets and that park a couple of blocks over. I doubt that she's there, but you might spot her in or near some of those shops near the park." Jamie glanced back toward Barbara. "Johnson knows what Mrs. Riley looks like, but it would help if he knew what she's wearing."

Quickly, Barbara described how Meg had been dressed. The man didn't comment; he simply shared one silent glance with Jamie and left. Jamie gestured to a chair. "I need to report this to Taylor," he said. "Unfortunately..." He hesitated a moment. "Unfortunately, we seem to have lost radio contact."

"Oh." Barbara's knees gave way and she sank onto a chair.

"We're not worried yet," Jamie said. "This sometimes happens."

"Sure," Barbara said.

Jamie did smile then, and the smile transformed him into the innocent tutor the girls had come to love. "You sounded just like Mickie. I wondered where she got that completely disbelieving inflection."

"He's gone to meet Truett, hasn't he?"

That surprised Jamie. "I thought you knew. But really," he said, regaining his composure and his innocent appearance, "there's no reason to worry. We know where they are. Our own men are in the area, as well as some federal officers. It's only a matter of time before they get out of whatever interference they've wandered into and we have voice contact again."

"He's walked into a trap, hasn't he?"

"No. The only trap out there is ours." Jamie put his hand on her shoulder but quickly drew it back. "Try not to worry," he told her.

Try not to worry. Chilled in the air-conditioned room, Barbara rubbed her arms through the long sleeves of her thin cotton shirt. Try not to worry when Zack was God alone knew where facing God alone knew what. Try not to worry while Meg had run out either to escape from or to confront someone, and Barbara was very much afraid she knew who that someone was. Even though she was unsuccessful in her efforts not to worry, Barbara sat quietly, listening to the hum of voices and the beeps and clicks of electronic equipment and the thud of her heartbeat roaring in her ears while Jamie and his crew monitored what they could, and waited. Waited for Zack to return. Waited for Meg to return. Waited for the moment when she had reached the limit of what she could endure and her sanity finally snapped.

"Jamie."

Barbara glanced up sharply at the concern in the voice of the man who stood at the opening in the partition. Jamie unplugged his headset and walked to the man, conferring with him quietly but with a great deal of animation, and when he turned to face her, Barbara saw that same concern written on Jamie's features.

"What is it?" she asked. "Is it Zack? Has something happened to him?"

"Barbara—"

"*What is it?*"

Jamie ran a hand through his hair and then plugged in his headset and keyed in a number on the console near the map. "It's the girls," he said.

"Mickie..."

"And Dianne. Hold on a moment while I make this report."

All she could do was hold on—to the arms of her uncomfortable chair, to the hysteria that threatened to overpower her—as Jamie tersely finished his report to someone at the other end of his electronic connection.

"The guard at the door saw them leave less than five minutes ago. He tried to stop them, but they jumped into a black-and-yellow taxi that seemed to be waiting for them, and it took off before he got an ID or tag number... Right... Right... Yes."

He looked at Barbara. "That was our contact at the FBI. In about thirty seconds every cop in Houston will be looking for those two girls. We *will* get them back all right."

Barbara dropped her head onto her hands. Her baby. And defenseless little Dianne. Out there. Alone. No. Not alone. At the mercy of a madman. She should have been with them. She should have stopped them. What kind of a mother was she to let her child walk into danger? She brought a knuckle to her mouth and bit down hard to keep from screaming out her guilt and her fear and her pain. And then she sat there quietly, holding her arms in a tight hug, rocking slightly, waiting, because there was nothing else she could do. And that inability to do anything was in itself still another kind of torture.

After what seemed an eternity, Barbara heard the murmur of voices from the outer room, but she didn't look up. What was the point? Everyone she loved was in danger, and regardless of this new crisis, she was as powerless to do anything as she had been when she, herself, had been held hostage. Was this how Zack had felt then? Oh, God, she would do *anything* to keep him from feeling this pain again.

"Barbara."

She dragged her head up to see Zack crouched in front of her, to see the same despair she felt mirrored in his eyes.

"You're safe," she whispered. "Oh, Zack, thank God, you're safe."

He pulled her from the chair, to her feet, and into his arms, and she wrapped her arms around him, needing to touch him, to feel the solid strength of him. "I thought he had you. When I heard they'd lost radio contact, I thought I'd never see you again."

"It's all right," he murmured against her hair. "I wasn't in danger. He didn't show up. I'm here now. I have you. It's all right."

But it wasn't. She stiffened in his arms and tried to pull away from him. "Mickie..."

"I know," he told her, and she heard anguish in his voice. "God in Heaven, I know.

"But we'll get her back," he said, resolve strengthening his words. "We'll get all of them back. But right now, let's get you upstairs."

She looked up then to see that they stood alone in that section of the room, with Jamie and Taylor stationed at the partition opening giving them privacy and protecting them from anyone else's accidental intrusion. Taylor—Taylor looked grim and ashen. "He has to be in agony, too," she said. Reluctantly releasing her grasp on Zack, she walked to Taylor's side. "I'm sorry," she said.

Taylor shook his head. "For what, Barbara? For my incompetence? Zack hired me to do a job, one I thought I was capable of doing. He has a staff of security experts that would be the envy of a small city, enough electronic surveillance equipment to go retail on a national level, and I can't even manage to keep one woman and two small children on the sixteenth floor of a secure building where they will be safe."

"That's because you designed it to keep people out, Taylor, not in," Zack told him. "We didn't build a jail, I wouldn't have had one."

"I think I know how the girls left, after Mickie's past escapades," Taylor said, either not hearing or not heeding Zack's attempt to reassure him. "But how did Meg leave? Did he get to one of our men?"

"The back stairs," Barbara told him, knowing he probably didn't want to hear how easy it had been for Meg to leave but also knowing he had to take precautions. "She . . . she learned the codes."

Taylor drew himself up and looked at Zack in resignation. Barbara recognized their silent message. If Meg could get out, she could tell anyone how to get in. "I'll have the codes changed right away."

Zack hugged her tighter to his side. "Yes." He looked over at Jamie. "And keep me advised of what's happening. I'll be upstairs with my wife."

Had she ever really been a wife to Zachary Gordon? Once Barbara would have said yes, early in their marriage, but as they rode upstairs in the elevator, as Zack briefed Mr. Tewksbury, as they walked in silence with Zack's arm still holding her to his side toward Mickie's room, she wondered if she hadn't simply been a child in a woman's body, playing at marriage. If not, wouldn't she be able to turn to him now and say *I need to be held, I need to be comforted. I need to be told that we'll all get through this unharmed?* Or maybe her inability to turn to Zack came not from her never having been his wife so much as the lengths she had gone to in her effort to make him forget that she had been.

Mickie's door was open. Her computer hummed, but some sort of wild, Star Wars screen saver danced across the monitor. The room was cluttered and untidy, in the way she had come to expect her child's room to be. Barbara raised her fist to her mouth, choking back a sob. Tesla lay curled and snoring in the center of Mickie's pillow.

"Why did she leave?" she moaned. "What on earth could have sent the two of them out, without a word to anyone?"

"Maybe not without a word," Zack told her, leading her into the room, toward the desk and a tented sheet of printer paper.

Mickie's spelling was far less sophisticated than her vocabulary, but the painstakingly printed message was legible.

Mom

   That dumb cockatoo is at the airport. We can't find
you or Meg and Dianne's going airborn herself because if somebody doesn't pick it up in an hour it's going back to Fenix. I took my piggybank money and
we'll be care full.[q

                                                    Love you,
                                                    Mickie

Barbara clutched the note. "Call Jamie."

"Not yet." Still not removing his arm from her shoulder,
Zack tapped a key on the computer, restoring the screen to
its last function, which was the telecommunications menu.

"Of course," Zack muttered. "Why in the hell didn't I
think of that before I gave her access to the outside world?"

"What do you mean?" Barbara demanded.

Zack released her and bent over the printer stand, dragging up sheets of paper from the back of the machine. "She
prints everything—I know that from her forays downstairs.
At least, I hope she still does. Damn!"

"Zack?"

"Now I'll call Jamie. And now I know how Taylor feels,
because *I* gave Wilson access to the girls. Through one of the
network services, Barbara, and the modem. And I'm very
much afraid that Meg, after *I* insisted that she be allowed to
go to that conference, gave him the information he needed
to make contact."

He dropped the paper onto the printer and grasped her by
the shoulders, leading her to the bed. "Sit here," he told
her, giving her a nudge until she sat on the edge of the bed.
"And here's something to hold on to until I get back," he
said, scooping up the cat and thrusting him into her arms.

"I'm just going to the nearest telephone," he said slowly
and distinctly. "I won't be far, and I won't be gone long."

She recognized why he was being so careful with her; he
thought she was about to break. "I'm all right," she insisted.

"No, you're not. Neither one of us is. But we will be, I promise you. Somehow, I'll make sure of that."

She held and stroked Tesla, realizing on some level that she did take comfort from the nearness of another living creature, until Zack returned, put the cat back on the pillow, and led her, unprotesting, to his room.

Once there, he closed the door behind them, leaned back against it, and drew Barbara into his arms, holding her fiercely, protectively, while she felt the tension thrumming through him.

"I love you," he said, speaking above her while he held her head to his chest. "I thought for years that would be the last thing you wanted to hear from me. For all those years, I thought—I thought you had probably made a new life for yourself, one in which you had forgotten me, if not the pain my loving you had caused you. These last few weeks, though, I had begun to hope that if I could prove to you that I could keep you safe, you might learn to trust me, and to love me again, and that we might have a future together in spite of the way I had failed you.

"Now I've put your child in jeopardy—"

"Not you—"

"And I had begun to see how futile my hope was. You have every right to hate me, Barbara—"

Hate him? Never. But the day's events had made her, too, see how futile and pitifully naive her own hopes had been.

"And when I came to you this afternoon, you had every right to lash out at me for the danger I had once again placed you in, that I had brought down on Mickie—"

"No—"

"But you didn't." Zack's arms tightened against her back, and he bent to rub his cheek against her hair. "You came into my arms, and you said, *you're safe,* and nothing will ever again make me believe you don't love me. So why, *why* won't you stay with me? Why would you put us through the hell of separation again? I'll get Mickie back for you. I promise. I'll get her back, and Wilson will never touch either of you again."

Could she tell him? Could she *not* tell him and let him continue to carry a guilt he should never have had to bear? "Zack—"

The telephone rang, interrupting what Barbara still didn't know she would say.

She heard Zack's muttered oath as he held her for only a second and then began releasing her. "I have to answer it."

"I know," she told him.

She felt his hands tighten briefly on her shoulder before he turned from her and crossed to the telephone, answering with no more than a terse "What?"

Now she leaned against the door, hugging herself tightly, rubbing her hands up her arms against the chill invading her as she waited for the news that had intruded on them.

"I want a head start," she heard Zack say. "I don't give a damn what *they* want, I want to get to him first. Fine. I'll be right down."

He replaced the telephone and turned, and Barbara didn't recognize the grim, determined man facing her across the width of the room.

"Mickie?" she asked, her voice faint, fear tightening her throat.

"She's all right. For now, at least. Johnson was a block away, searching for Meg, when a taxi passed him. The girls were in the back seat, Mickie apparently shouting at the driver. He recognized the driver, too. It was... It was Wilson. Johnson had taken his personal car because all of ours were out on the wild-goose chase Wilson had led us on earlier, so he didn't have a phone with him. But he followed them until he was sure of their destination...."

She wasn't aware of him moving, but suddenly he was in front of her. "I'll bring her back to you, Barbara. I'll give you that, if I can give you nothing else."

"No!" On some instinctual level, Barbara knew she couldn't let him leave without her; that if he did, she might never see him again.

"No?"

"No," she said. "You won't bring her back to me because I'm going with you."

"Barbara, it's not safe for you to go with me."

She laughed bitterly, surprising even herself. "Everyone I love is in danger," she said. "Do you think I care about being *safe?* No," she said, interrupting him as he started to speak. "The only way you can leave me behind is to lock me up, and you won't do that to me, will you, Zack?"

Thirteen

She wouldn't let go of his hand. Zack felt the pressure of Barbara's slender, strong fingers clutching his as his efficient driver wound through Houston traffic, down into the tunnel, across bridges and overpasses. Jamie sat beside the driver, coordinating their actions over the cellular phone. Taylor sat on the other side of Barbara, while others followed in a caravan, toward a confrontation that should have taken place years ago.

Zack felt another pressure, that of the .357 against his back. For the second time in his life, he understood the depths of hatred. For the second time in his life, he knew that if he had the opportunity he would use that deadly little revolver to snuff out the life of another person with no more regret than he would have for a rabid animal.

He looked down at their clasped hands. She was all that was precious in life to him. Nothing else really mattered; not the company, not the buildings, not the penthouse, not the power or the wealth that made this caravan possible—or necessary.

She looked up at him, and he wanted to fold her into his arms, hide her face against his chest so that he didn't have to see her enormous, bruised-looking eyes, or her beautiful features from which all color had been leeched. Instead, he looked again at their clasped hands. She wouldn't let go of his hand. Or maybe *he* wouldn't let go of hers.

"What is this place?" Barbara asked, and Zack realized the car had turned off the highway and was approaching the entrance to a large, gulf-side compound surrounded by an ancient, well-battered, chain-link fence.

"It's been a lot of things." Taylor spoke for the first time since leaving the penthouse. "At one time, it was a yacht-building yard. A later owner tried a private marina with hopes for a major hotel. For the last dozen or so years it's been tied up in bankruptcy court and pretty much abandoned."

The car pulled to a stop at the open gate, and a man stepped from the derelict gatehouse and approached the driver's door. Zack recognized Johnson, one of Taylor's staff, when Taylor lowered his window.

"They're still here?" Taylor asked.

Johnson nodded as he shifted position to face Taylor. "On the old yacht at the end of the far pier."

"Are they all right?" Zack asked.

"The girls seem to be. Scared, of course. He carried Mrs. Riley on board, though, and I couldn't tell if it was because she was bound or unconscious."

"Zack," Jamie said, extending the cellular phone toward him. "Truett's on the line to the office, asking to speak to you."

Zack took the phone. "Patch him through," he said.

"Hello, brother, dear." Wilson's voice grated down his spine, chilling him. "I congratulate you on having a much more efficient staff than I had thought possible, but I believe I have something you want."

"Name your price."

Zack felt Barbara's fingers clench on his.

"No," Wilson told him. "We negotiate face-to-face or not at all."

The demand didn't surprise Zack. Hadn't he realized this meeting was inevitable? "I suppose you want me to come on board."

Wilson's laugh broke off in a cough. "Oh, yes," he said. "You, and your lovely wife, and I believe that fine, upstanding Mr. Adams."

"No." The word erupted from him. What the hell was Wilson up to now?

"No? Oh, yes. You are the supplicants, therefore you must come to me—your lovely wife because she wants her daughter, Mr. Adams because he wants the beautiful Mrs. Riley, and you because...because at last you want to kill me, and you know that you will never get another chance."

Zack pressed the telephone mouthpiece against his thigh to muffle his words. "How much time do we have?" he asked Jamie.

"Too much," Jamie said, affirming what Zack already suspected. They'd been too generous in the time they'd allowed themselves before law enforcement officers arrived. "Stall him."

"I don't like this setup, Zack," Taylor said, echoing Zack's thoughts even though he didn't know yet of the demands. "It makes no sense for him to risk being trapped in this basin."

He felt Barbara's free hand brush across his cheek. "What do we have to do?" she asked.

No amount of arguing persuaded her to stay out of danger. The pier was too unsound to risk driving on, so the three of them, flanked by half a dozen of his men, walked to the end of the pier, to a yacht that had undoubtedly once been someone's pride but now seemed barely substantial enough to stay afloat in the security of the basin.

A wide, makeshift plank stretched between the pier and the opening to the deck. Zack looked at it for several seconds before turning and taking Barbara in his arms. "Stay here," he whispered in her ear, having to try at least one more time. "Faint, have hysterics, do anything, *something,* but for God's sake, don't get on that boat."

"Zack—" He felt her arms go around him, felt the moment she discovered the gun tucked in his belt. He heard her small hiss of surprise, felt her arms tighten around him, and he knew she wouldn't stay on the pier.

"Touching."

He looked up to see Wilson standing on the deck beside the gangplank, holding Mickie in front of him.

Zack heard Barbara's faint moan when she, too, saw her daughter.

"Hurry up," Wilson said, "before this—"

"Mom, I'm sorry. I really am. I didn't know—"

"Shut up, brat. Are you three coming on board or not? Or do I have to throw this kid in the gulf?"

"No!" Mickie cried out, and Zack swore he had never heard anyone sound more terrified. "Please don't throw me in. Oh, please, don't." *Mickie? Terrified of water?*

Zack shared one long questioning glance with Barbara before they turned to the gangplank. Taylor went first, then Barbara, then Zack.

"Now," Truett said, gesturing toward Taylor with his automatic when all three were finally on board. "Toss that plank over the side and tell your men to back off."

While Taylor did as he was told, Zack stepped next to Barbara and put his arm over her shoulder, in part to keep her from charging toward Mickie, in part so that he could fend off any attack directed at her.

"How charming," Truett said, then motioned once again with his weapon. "Shall we go forward?"

When they followed his directions, they found Dianne unbound but huddled on the rust-pocked deck next to a gaping hole in the railing. Zack saw no sign of Meg.

"Are you all right, Dianne?" Barbara asked.

"Quiet! Don't you want me to tell you how easy it was to get you all out of the compound? Don't you want to know how I managed to know when and how and what to taunt you with? Don't you want to know why Ms. Riley took you in and how she got the money for Dianne's operations? And you, Mr. Adams? Don't you want to know what I've done with the beautiful Ms. Riley, for whom you have developed such an affection?''

"You bastard," Taylor muttered.

"Quite possibly. My mother wasted no time in remarrying after my father's death, so it's possible she wasn't faithful to him in life, either, isn't that right, brother, dear?''

Zack had wondered why Wilson hated him but had never dreamed the roots of that hatred went back so far. "Your mother was a beautiful woman, Wilson, in appearance and in character. She would never have betrayed a commitment."

"No?" Wilson shrugged as though tired of the subject. "Perhaps not. But perhaps neither she nor that father you think so much of were of quite as high a moral fiber as you seem to be Zack. Perhaps we have more in common than *step*parents."

No way. Zack rejected the insinuation. He remembered his mother; he remembered how his father had loved her; he remembered the values both his parents had lived by. He also remembered Wilson's tawdry little lies about teachers and the household staff. What his mind couldn't come up with was a reason for Wilson to be making these allegations now.

"Where is Meg?"

Zack heard Taylor's softly growled demand, but Wilson ignored it, smiling slightly as he shifted his hold on Mickie, pushing her closer to the hole in the railing. "I think it's time to get rid of the children. They can be such a bother, can't they?''

"Oh, God, no," he heard Barbara moan.

"Why, Wilson?" he asked. "What do you want?"

"Nothing," Wilson said. "Nothing you can give me. Except maybe satisfaction for what you have taken."

"You can't get that by hurting the girls," Barbara cried. "They have no hold on him. *She's not his daughter!*"

"Better and better," Truett muttered, jerking Mickie around to face Zack. "What about it? Doesn't she have some hold on you?" he asked.

Zack stared into Mickie's eyes. *What about it?* Her only chance lay with him lying about how much she had come to mean to him. But if he denied it, would she ever forgive him? If he didn't, would she live to forgive him? He had no choice. Taylor stood to one side of him, partially blocking Truett's view. Zack gripped Barbara's arm with one hand to keep her from lunging forward, while with the other he reached for the gun in his belt. "Go ahead," he said, silently trying to convince Mickie that he meant just the opposite of what he said. "She's nothing to me."

"Water, I think," Truett muttered. "Or should I just shoot her?" And Zack knew his lie had failed. He stood in helpless futility while Truett edged Mickie closer to the hole in the railing. But instead of looking away, Mickie continued to stare at Zack's face. "No. She's terrified of the water. I never heard a brat scream more than these two when I carried them over the plank."

Good for you, Mickie, Zack thought, at last understanding why she had cried out earlier though surely Wilson would have seen them swimming over the years. Now if only Mickie could understand what *he* was trying to do. Almost as though he had spoken aloud to her, she started to cry.

"No," Zack called out. "Not that, please, no."

Wilson laughed softly, triumphantly, and Zack realized he had only thought he knew the depths of hatred; he hadn't until now, until he saw it glittering without reason or rationality from Wilson's eyes. Still laughing, Wilson shoved Mickie at the same time he released his grasp on her and sent her tumbling over the side of the boat.

Barbara screamed, an unfeigned, unrehearsed, very real scream of pain and terror for her child, and Zack felt it in each and every bone and nerve ending in his body. *Be safe, Mickie.* He sent his thoughts silently to the valiant little girl who had stolen her way into his heart, but then returned to the very real danger facing Barbara—and himself.

"Now for the lovely wife," Wilson said, turning his gun toward Barbara.

Hatred? No. What Zack saw in Wilson's eyes went beyond hatred. To—*evil?* Zack had acknowledged believing in it, but did he really? Or was this virulence shooting toward him from Wilson's eyes the product of nothing other than insanity?

"Aren't you going to do anything, Zack? Are you just going to let me kill your whole family?"

Zack had his hand on the revolver now, easing it from the belt. He saw the dare in Wilson's eyes, heard the taunt in his voice, felt the anticipation in his stance, and knew in an instant what Wilson wanted—more than life, more than power—he wanted Zack to kill him. But why? What would he gain? Except perhaps the final destruction of Zachary Gordon. Zack pushed that thought away. If anyone deserved to die, it was Wilson Truett. If anyone had a right to kill, it was he, Zack, for all the pain, for all the wrongs, for all the threats, past, present, and in the future if Wilson wasn't stopped.

Thank God, you were not the one to have to kill someone. I don't think I could live with myself if you had been brought to that because of me.

Too clearly, Zack remembered the words of Barbara's letter. Could she live with it now?

"She really is a loyal little thing," Wilson said, nodding toward Barbara. "I told her I would break you eventually, and that she would be my means. It really was considerate of you, Zack, to let yourself be vulnerable like that, but, oh, so inconsiderate of her to leave you. I do believe she thought it would make a difference, that somehow you would stop caring enough to be safe. Foolish, wasn't she? Especially when it was so easy for me to keep track of her, so easy for me to see that you found her when I decided the time was right."

Was that why she had left? Not out of fear for herself, but out of fear for him? With a quick, shocked glance at her, Zack saw the truth of Wilson's accusation in her expressive eyes, and saw the moment when she realized he at last knew the truth. *Oh, Barbara,* he thought through this new pain. *How much has this madman stolen from us?*

He caught a glimpse of motion from the corner of his eye and saw Dianne creeping toward the hole in the railing.

Stall, he thought. Give her time to escape before all hell breaks loose on the deck.

"Why, Wilson? Can you at least tell me why you've done all this?"

Wilson lifted his lips in a parody of a smile and yet also in suggestion of a triumphant leer. "No, I don't think I will."

Perhaps because he couldn't? Zack wondered. Perhaps because there *was* no reason, no rationale, no sanity in this man's actions. His eyes taunted him. *You can't kill me, can you? No matter what I do?*

Could he? And if he did, alien as the thought might be, did Wilson win? Win what? Trapped in a ship basin with federal officers due to arrive any moment, surrounded by Zack's own men, he couldn't hope to escape. And Wilson had set it up. Intended to be here, in this way, at this time. Why?

"You've got no backbone, have you, Zack?" Wilson taunted. "No heart for killing, no matter what provocation? No heart for protecting what's yours? No blood lust? Surely you do."

Zack saw that Dianne had reached the opening but had hesitated. *No blood lust?* When what he wanted more than anything at this moment was to see Wilson bleeding and suffering? No, that wasn't true. What he wanted more than anything was to have Wilson out of his life, to forget he had ever existed. But if he killed him, neither he nor Barbara would ever be free of him. And he knew at that moment that he might die, but that he wouldn't kill Wilson and that Wilson would never again be free to torture him or anyone else.

"Jump, Dianne!" he yelled, and in the moment Wilson stood stunned into immobility by the fragile little girl's neat dive over the side of the boat, Zack abandoned any thought of the gun in his belt and leapt across the deck in a long, diving tackle, catching Wilson off-balance and sending him thudding to the deck.

In an anticlimax worthy of Hollywood, the coast guard, the FBI and the police arrived en masse only moments after

Zack and Taylor finished subduing Wilson Truett, only moments after the girls, who had swum around the yacht and been retrieved from the water by Jamie and crew, had run on board across the newly rigged gangplank and into Barbara's arms. She looked over her daughter's head and into Zack's shadowed eyes when the officers swarmed on board. She dared a small smile, which Zack did not return, and when the girls wriggled free from her embrace, he did not reach for them. Instead he spoke to Dianne, asking where Meg was, and followed the girl as she led the group of men below deck to the cabin where her mother had been held prisoner.

Uninvited, but not forbidden, Barbara followed, too. Meg's eyes found her from across the room, pleading for understanding as Taylor took the gag from her mouth and untied her wrists and ankles.

Could she understand? This woman had been her friend for seven years. Could she have deliberately betrayed her? No. Barbara knew that without having to rationalize anything. But could she forgive Meg for putting everyone she loved in such danger?

"He told me he was your husband," Meg said softly, speaking to Barbara even though others stood closer. "Seven years ago. He said he had hurt you, inadvertently, and knew why you left, but that he loved you and wanted to look after you. He offered me help with Dianne's medical bills if I helped him, if I gave you the job. But I believed him. I still believed him when he suggested it would be more convenient for Dianne if we moved to Houston, to be near the medical facilities.

"Until Zack showed up. Until I began to realize who *Mr. Smith* really was.

"And then I couldn't get free from him. I tried. Please believe, I tried."

She turned to Zack. "He wanted you to kill him. He told me that much. He told me he'd never left the country, just gone into hiding with the help of the money he'd gotten from selling the plans he'd taken from you. And that he hadn't really known what he would do with Barbara all those years while he kept track of her, but that he thought she might be of some use—'' Meg's voice broke, but she struggled to continue. "Might be of some use at a later date. Which...which she was, when he learned that if ever he was going to destroy you, he had to move quickly.

"He has cancer, Zack. Of the stomach. He's dying. But he wanted *you* to be the one who killed him."

Barbara sat on the edge of Mickie's bed, absently stroking Tesla's fur. The room was dim, with only the night-light burning, only a thin stream of light coming from the partially open bathroom door.

She had forced herself to leave Mickie alone to finish her bath, knowing her daughter was becoming increasingly uncomfortable with her mother's attention. But Barbara couldn't help it. She had almost lost her daughter today, and if she was within touching distance of her, she would touch her, would hug her, would embarrass her with the love she had to voice.

She heard the hall door open and looked up to see Zack standing in the doorway, at last free from statements and interrogation and the police. Silently she lifted Tesla, placing him on the pillow, and stood. Just as silently, Zack crossed the room, stopping a single step away from her, not speaking...waiting.

How did she choose? How did she reconcile her love for Mickie and her love for Zack? And did she have to? Today he had been prepared to give his life for her child. Surely, somehow, they could weave the fabrics of their lives into a loving whole... They had to, because in that time when Barbara had been faced with losing Zack, she had realized she could never again survive being separated from him.

"That was why you left, wasn't it?" he asked softly. "Because you thought I'd be safer with you gone."

She bit at her lip, unable to answer.

"Tell me, Barbara, if Mickie ran away, would you stop loving her?"

"No," she whispered.

"Would you stop wanting to have her with you?"

She shook her head.

"Would you be any less vulnerable, any less concerned about her safety? Would you forget her?"

She couldn't answer him, and she knew she didn't have to.

"Then why did you think I could forget you?"

Yes, why? she asked herself. Once, long ago, it had seemed so clear to her. Now she knew how futile her attempt to protect him had been. But until Zack, and now Mickie, she had never been loved or been able to give her love. Could Zack ever forgive her for not knowing *how* to love?

"You're staying with me," he said. "There's no way in hell I'm ever again going through the agony of losing you."

She glanced up, meeting the shadows and questions in his eyes, and took that one step forward that committed her to Zack and to his love.

She felt a deep sigh escape him before his arms went around her, holding her—just holding her, as though she were the most precious thing in his life.

They stood there in silence for only seconds. Too much had happened, too much still must be said. Barbara stepped back, and Zack let her go, but she raised her hand to his cheek.

"Meg?" she asked.

"Taylor has taken her and Dianne to their house. I've given him some time off to be with them. There won't be any charges filed against her. She was a victim, too, Barbara."

Barbara nodded. In her heart she knew that. "I'm glad she'll have someone with her. And . . . and Wilson?"

"In jail, but it's doubtful he'll live long enough to stand trial on any of the charges."

She absorbed that information silently but with a small shudder. "And you, Zack?" she asked.

"I'm— No. I won't be all right until we resolve what still stands between us." He lifted his hands to her shoulders but did not attempt to draw her closer. "Wilson has taken so much from us that we can never recover, but we must not give him any more than he has already taken. We have to find a way to go forward from here, free of him and his hatred. Can we do that, Barbara?''

Could they? Barbara had few doubts that they could, except for one very important part of her life.

She heard the water gurgling down the drain of the tub, heard a happy childish voice singing, and then saw the room lighten as Mickie opened the bathroom door and came into the bedroom all scrubbed and fresh and dressed for bed. She stopped singing when she saw Zack and walked solemnly toward him. Barbara stepped back, giving her room to approach, and watched as Mickie and Zack looked into each other's eyes, exchanging silent questions.

''I almost believed you,'' Mickie said in her little-girl-trying-to-be-adult voice. ''When Mom told that man I wasn't your daughter, when you told him you didn't care if he killed me, I almost believed you. Until you started begging him not to throw me in the water. It was like poker, wasn't it—when you don't have any good cards in your hand but you want the other players to think you do? It was a bluff, wasn't it?''

Zack dropped to his knees in front of her, and Barbara saw the moisture glistening in his eyes. ''Yes, Mickie,'' he told her. ''It was a bluff, like you letting Truett think you were afraid of the water. But what Wilson didn't know was that with you and your mom and love at my side, I'll always have the winning hand.

''And I think it's time to answer a question you asked me a long time ago, a question your mom wasn't free to answer then. Remember the day we met, when you were taking care of a whole houseful of sick people. You asked me if I was your father.''

Through eyes blurred with tears, Barbara watched Mickie nod solemnly.

''Yes, Mickie, I am,'' Zack said thickly. ''And I am very, very proud of you.'' He gave her an awkward hug, releasing her with obvious reluctance. ''But now I think it's time for me and your mom to tuck you in so you can get some sleep.''

Mickie nodded and hopped up onto the bed, nudging Tesla to one side and under the sheet. ''I thought you were. I hoped you were.'' Looking up, she studied Barbara for a second. ''Why are you crying, Mom?'' she asked.

Barbara wiped at her eyes and managed a watery chuckle. ''Because I'm happy, darling.''

''Good,'' Mickie told her, scooting down under the sheet. ''It's about time.''

''Are you happy, Barbara?'' Zack asked when they closed the door to his room behind them.

Barbara leaned against Zack, letting him enfold her, nodding against his chest.

She hadn't thought it possible she could love Zack more, but she did, and she knew there was something she had to do—had to give him—if there was any chance at all of it being true.

''We'll have her tested,'' she said. ''You deserve to know if she is your daughter.''

With gentle pressure, Zack pulled away from her and held her motionless. ''No. You were right about not running the risk of branding her. The child she is, is all the truth I need, because that child is pretty wonderful.

''But someday—not just yet because I think we need some time together to heal, but soon—we need to think about making another baby.'' He chuckled, and Barbara felt the tension leaving him, leaving her. He pulled her against him, now speaking with the teasing, loving banter she had not heard since that night in Charleston a lifetime before and had not thought she would ever hear again.

''Maybe a son this time,'' he said. ''Remember, we'd planned for a little girl that looks like you and a little boy that looks like me. But we didn't make any provision for intelligence, and it isn't fair to you that the one child we already have has my brains.''

Epilogue

Barbara moaned once in protest, trying to hold on to the fading images of her dream. She lay still for a moment after awakening, willing them to return. When they didn't, she sighed and stretched and pulled herself up against the headboard, taking sheet and blanket with her.

She thought again, as she had long ago, about the symbolism of dreams, but this time she smiled as she looked out over the moon-washed bedroom.

She heard the change in breathing that told her Zack was awakening, that as always, even in sleep, he was aware when she left his side.

"Bad dream?" he asked, concerned, reaching for her.

"Oh, no," she whispered, going into his arms, letting him pull her against his sleep-warm body. "Not at all."

Once she had promised herself she would stop running, that she would rebuild her life, that she would find a place that could be her home. But she had never suspected that all three of those goals would meet in one place—

Here. In Zachary Gordon's arms. But only after she had allowed herself to love him and to accept the love he had never stopped giving her.

"As a matter of fact," she said, trailing her fingers over his chest and laughing in soft satisfaction, "it was such a good dream, I think I ought to share it with you."

Zack caught her hand, stilling it, holding it against his heart. "That good, was it?" he asked, nuzzling his lips against her throat. "As good as the real thing?"

"Oh, no," Barbara conceded quickly. "No dream could ever be that good."

She heard Zack's satisfied chuckle.

"But almost," she told him.

He growled a mock threat and lifted himself to one elbow, leaning over her. "Then maybe you'd better share it with me."

"Oh, I will, my darling," she said softly. "Yes, I certainly will."

* * * * *

Stories that capture living and loving beneath the Big Sky, where legends live on...and mystery lingers.

This January, the intrigue continues with

OUTLAW LOVERS
by Pat Warren

He was a wanted man. She was the beckoning angel who offered him a hideout. Now their budding passion has put them both in danger. And he'd do anything to protect her.

Don't miss a minute of the loving as the passion continues with:

> **WAY OF THE WOLF**
> by Rebecca Daniels (February)
>
> **THE LAW IS NO LADY**
> by Helen R. Myers (March)
>
> **FATHER FOUND**
> by Laurie Paige (April)
> and many more!

Only from ▼ *Silhouette*® where passion lives.

Bestselling Author

Elise Title

Anything less than everything is not enough.

Coming in January 1995, Sylver Cassidy and Kate Paley take
on the movers and shakers of Hollywood. Young, beautiful,
been-there, done-it-all type women, they're ready to live by their
own rules and stand by their own mistakes. With love on the
horizon, can two women bitten by the movie bug really have it
all? Find out in

HOT
PROPERTY

SILHOUETTE®
Desire®

MAN of the MONTH 1995

Don't let the winter months get you down because the heat is about to get turned way up...with the sexiest hunks of 1995!

January: *A NUISANCE*
by Lass Small

February: *COWBOYS DON'T CRY*
by Anne McAllister

March: *THAT BURKE MAN*
the 75th Man of the Month
by Diana Palmer

April: *MR. EASY*
by Cait London

May: *MYSTERIOUS MOUNTAIN MAN*
by Annette Broadrick

June: *SINGLE DAD*
by Jennifer Greene

**MAN OF THE MONTH...
ONLY FROM
SIILHOUETTE DESIRE**

MOM95JJ-R

Beginning next month from

SILHOUETTE® *Desire*®

FROM HERE TO MATERNITY

by Elizabeth Bevarly

A new series celebrating the unexpected joys of motherhood—and fatherhood!

Three single women each meet the man of their dreams…and receive a precious surprise package from a certain stork.

In February—
A DAD LIKE DANIEL (#908)

In April—
THE PERFECT FATHER (#920)

In June—
DR. DADDY (#933)

Watch these soon-to-be moms as they are swept off their feet and into the maternity ward!
Only from Silhouette Desire.

Robert...Luke...Noah
Three proud, strong brothers who live—and
love—by

THE CODE OF THE WEST

Meet the Tanner man, starting with
Silhouette Desire's *Man of the Month* for
February, Robert Tanner, in Anne McAllister's

COWBOYS DON'T CRY

Robert Tanner never let any woman get close
to him—especially not Maggie MacLeod. But
the tempting new owner of his ranch was
determined to get past the well-built defenses
around his heart....

And be sure to watch for brothers Luke and Noah,
in their own stories, COWBOYS DON'T QUIT
and COWBOYS DON'T STAY, throughout 1995!

Only from

SILHOUETTE... **Where Passion Lives**

Don't miss these Silhouette favorites by some of our most distinguished authors! And now you can receive a discount by ordering two or more titles!

SD#05786	QUICKSAND by Jennifer Greene	$2.89	☐
SD#05795	DEREK by Leslie Guccione	$2.99	☐
SD#05818	NOT JUST ANOTHER PERFECT WIFE		
	by Robin Elliott	$2.99	☐
IM#07505	HELL ON WHEELS by Naomi Horton	$3.50	☐
IM#07514	FIRE ON THE MOUNTAIN		
	by Marion Smith Collins	$3.50	☐
IM#07559	KEEPER by Patricia Gardner Evans	$3.50	☐
SSE#09879	LOVING AND GIVING by Gina Ferris	$3.50	☐
SSE#09892	BABY IN THE MIDDLE	$3.50 U.S.	☐
	by Marie Ferrarella	$3.99 CAN.	☐
SSE#09902	SEDUCED BY INNOCENCE	$3.50 U.S.	☐
	by Lucy Gordon	$3.99 CAN.	☐
SR#08952	INSTANT FATHER by Lucy Gordon	$2.75	☐
SR#08984	AUNT CONNIE'S WEDDING		
	by Marie Ferrarella	$2.75	☐
SR#08990	JILTED by Joleen Daniels	$2.75	☐

(limited quantities available on certain titles)

AMOUNT		$_____
DEDUCT: 10% DISCOUNT FOR 2+ BOOKS		$_____
POSTAGE & HANDLING		$_____
($1.00 for one book, 50¢ for each additional)		
APPLICABLE TAXES*		$_____
TOTAL PAYABLE		$_____
(check or money order—please do not send cash)		

To order, complete this form and send it, along with a check or money order for the total above, payable to Silhouette Books, to: **In the U.S.:** 3010 Walden Avenue, P.O. Box 9077, Buffalo, NY 14269-9077; **In Canada:** P.O. Box 636, Fort Erie, Ontario, L2A 5X3.

Name:_____

Address: _____ City:_____

State/Prov.:_____ Zip/Postal Code:_____

*New York residents remit applicable sales taxes.
Canadian residents remit applicable GST and provincial taxes.   SBACK-DF

◆ *Silhouette®*
™